NEW YORK

LUKE RICHARDSON

1

There are moments in life when the present leaves the past behind. It's as though the sharp knife of a surgeon cuts one from the other. Things divide neatly at these moments. They reinvent themselves in a wave of paradigm-shifting realisations. The world turns on a different axis and the old you stands there, motionless and watching, as the new you walks on into the unknown.

He turned his face to the sky. Light rain peppered his skin. The wet swish of tyres on tarmac sounded distant here. The city was quiet. He tightened his grip and the flow of blood slowed. It had pounded over his fingers. Now, it barely even dribbled.

He gazed down at the woman. At her eyes, still, and like marbles. Her skin, smooth as satin. Her mouth, an expressionless circle. The gash in her neck was the only thing that proved to him she was not simply resting.

The knife had also separated him from his past self. He was now a killer. A murderer. *Her* murderer.

The blade felt cold between his fingers. He lifted it to his face. Although the dripping blood was barely visible in the shadows, he could smell it. It was nourishing and fresh, like rain in the jungle.

His tongue flicked out between wet lips.

He longed to consume her. To make her a part of him. As he had now, and would always be, a part of her. She'd made a sacrifice for him. Now, in death, he would honour that. She was his first.

He was suddenly alert. Voices echoed down the passageway.

No, not like this.

He couldn't be discovered now. He needed time. He must have time to finish the job.

A group of people passed the passage's entrance on the road ahead. He watched them. He felt exposed. It was as though the world, once again, was trying to take away what was his.

The intruders' coats glistened beneath streetlights. None looked into the darkened passage. Why would they? Margins of the city like this held no interest. People were predictable.

They wouldn't even notice the narrow alley nestled beside the bright lights of the building next door.

It was the perfect location. Mansel Buck M.D. was the city's most prominent cosmetic surgeon. Those with fame and fortune passed through a set of brightly-lit doors daily for a nip, tuck, or whatever else was in vogue right now. No one would see down here. Not tonight.

The voices faded away into the whisper of the city. He drew a breath. No one had seen him. That was good. Yet, he didn't have much time. Time was the enemy here. Time had almost prevented his great-grandfather from fulfilling his artistic desires. That would not happen to him.

He pulled up his left sleeve. His great-grandfather's gold chain glinted beneath some distant light.

"This is for you," he whispered, placing the chain against his lips. It tasted like blood. "It's all for you."

Then he dropped to his knees and unbuttoned her coat.

2

The St Lucian sun crept towards the Caribbean Sea. The day had been calm but hot. It was precisely the sort of day the locals in the markets of Castries hated. Making their way home for dinner or a swift drink at the rum shop, they fanned the heat away with menus, newspapers or even their fingers.

The pool at St James' Bay, which an hour before had been filled with the shouts and splashes of children, grew quiet with the dying day. The calm water rippled gently, reflecting the surrounding palm trees.

"This looks alright," Leo said, walking to the pool's edge. He dropped his bag and glanced around. His reflection glittered on the surface of the pool. His baggy green t-shirt was creased and sweat-mottled from their journey across this island, and he desperately needed a haircut.

"It'll do," Allissa said, her reflection joining Leo's in the pool. She stared out at the gently rippling ocean. She wore a bright blue strappy top and baggy, yellow Alibaba pants.

"Get ready for your first swimming lesson." Allissa turned to face Leo.

"Not tonight," Leo whined. "We've only just got here. Let's just go to the bar and relax."

"No," Allissa asserted, "it's not like we've had a strenuous day. And you said last week that when we'd finished the case, you'd practise swimming every day."

"Yeah, so we'll start tomorrow."

"No." Allissa forced Leo's key card into his hands. "We'll start now. Go drop off your bag, get your shorts and meet me back here in ten." Allissa stepped towards the block which housed their adjacent rooms. "I'm not saving your arse every time there's water involved." Allissa walked away, a smile threatening to break across her face.

Leo cursed quietly and smiled too. He would be in the water within ten minutes — there was no point arguing with Allissa once she'd made her mind up.

Leo let himself into his room, dropped his bag and changed quickly.

Staying on in St Lucia was a good idea. They'd arrived ten days ago to gather information about a man who lived in a mansion on the island's northern coast. The man's wife had hired them after she'd become suspicious of the time he was spending on the island.

Leo and Allissa had watched the millionaire for a while, and noticed a glamourous woman visiting him every day. They reported this back to the wife, and she called the whole thing off. Perhaps she had enough information, or maybe she realised she didn't want to know exactly what her husband was doing. Either way, Leo and Allissa had been paid handsomely to come to the island. Now they wanted to make the most of it. They'd found this resort with two available rooms and headed straight here.

Leo draped a towel around his shoulders and padded back down to the pool. It was a nice place.

Leo dropped his towel on a sun lounger and gazed down at the pool's menacing ripples. His mouth felt dry and anxiety thumped in his throat. He forced himself to look away. People sat at the bar, laughing and joking. There was no threat here. He was in no danger.

Leo balled his fists, pulled a deep breath, and sat on the pool's edge. The water lapped across his legs. He slipped into the pool and stood up. The water only came up to his waist. His anxiety spiked again.

A flurry of laugher erupted from people at the nearby bar.

Why do I have to be doing this now? Leo mused morosely.

But then, something caught his eye and took his breath away.

3

Now that she was dead, he wondered, how should he refer to her?

He never knew her name, anyway. Maybe he should find out. She probably had some ID. His hands hovered above her handbag, discarded on the concrete.

No. He resisted the urge to look. There wasn't time for that. Besides, he would find out from the news tomorrow.

Moments like this were precious. He needed to make the most of them. She had died so that he could have this time. He owed it to her sacrifice.

He slid his hands beneath her clothes. He cursed the need to wear gloves. He wanted to feel her. To sense each ripple of her skin. Her body was still warm. That was good.

The body — he corrected himself. He should probably call it *the body* now. It wasn't hers anymore. Although, if he felt pedantic, maybe he should call it *his body* now? He'd created it, after all.

He smiled.

It was difficult to slide the raincoat from her limp arms. He put the knife down and used both hands to twist the raincoat from her. He thought of those mannequins in shops with the removable arms and head so they could be easily dressed. Maybe that's what he needed to do here.

He peered at the knife, blood dripping from the blade and fanning across the floor.

"Come on, come on," he whispered, weaving her limp arms from the sleeves.

The rain fell harder now. It ran from his face and inside his coat. It slipped over his back and chest. He didn't care. For a moment he thought of that rainy London autumn all those years ago. It would have felt just like this. He smiled with excitement.

Her thick jumper was already wet. Water had soaked into her clothes when she fell. It didn't matter. He picked up the knife and slid it carefully inside the jumper. He didn't want to cut the skin. Yet.

He sliced through the fabric and peeled the garment away. Only her bra remained. He felt a flurry of excitement. *The body. His body.*

He pulled the bra away from her skin and cut it. Again, he was careful not to penetrate the skin.

Blood from the ugly gash on her neck had run inside her clothes. He rubbed his hands through it. Blood smeared across her pale skin. She was cooling. He had to work quickly.

Starting at her neck, he traced a line with the knife across her body. His eyes closed. Power welled through him. When the knife reached her belly, he applied pressure. The soft skin fought back for a moment, dipping beneath the pressure of the blade, as though trying to hold back the tides. Then the skin yielded, and let his knife sink deep within it.

There was no blood now. All the blood had spilled already.

He increased pressure on the knife. It sunk another inch into her accommodating flesh.

Then he heard it. It didn't sound like much against the drumming of the rain and murmur of the city, but it was enough to pull him from his trance.

His head whipped from left to right. Mansel Buck M. D's Cosmetic Surgery had closed hours ago. No one had any business coming down here tonight.

He heard it again. Movement. He turned and gazed back towards the street.

A figure cast a silhouette against the glaring lights of the road. It moved closer.

He sprung to his feet and turned.

The stooped figure slouched closer.

This was not part of the plan.

He gripped the knife. He could kill again, of course. But that wasn't the way things were done.

"Just trying to get out of the rain," the figure said. A murmuring singsong hissed through toothless gums. Words slurred by drugs or madness. "It'll be nice to get home. Get warm."

The figure sidled further into the alley. The intruder hadn't seen him yet.

He looked back at the body. *His body.*

Her pale skill glowed ethereally in the gloom. *An angel.*

He didn't want to give up his prize. She was beautiful, but tainted now.

The ecstasy of the kill drained away. He couldn't get caught on the first one. That wasn't the way it was supposed to go.

Next time.

He pulled the hood of his raincoat low over his eyes, concealed the knife within his sleeve, and pushed past the figure.

"Oh sorry," the figure mumbled as he passed. "Just trying to get out of the rain."

He would have to start again. Then he would finish the job.

4

Leo and Allissa were close. They'd spent most of the last two years in each other's company. They both lived in and worked from their humble flat in Brighton. The definition of exactly what they did for a living was still up for discussion. Essentially, they found missing people around the world.

Their friendship had highs — when they rescued someone, or when the work was going well. And, naturally, lows — when they faced danger from some of the world's most awful people.

Leo had become used to sharing his life with Allissa. They travelled together, slept in adjoining rooms, in twin beds or next to each other on the aeroplane. Or rather, Allissa slept soundly on the aeroplane while Leo wished he could. Leo was used to that. And if he was honest, he liked it. He really liked it.

There was just one thing that Leo couldn't get used to. An uninvited urge that threatened to ruin it all. And, sure enough, as Allissa sauntered towards the pool in her red bikini, the unwelcome sensation surged again.

"You ready?" Allissa asked, crossing to Leo. Leo looked up at her from the shallow end.

"Yeah, sure," he said, shaking himself into focus. "I think so."

Allissa slid into the pool, floating effortlessly. The water lapped around her.

Leo held his arms above the water.

"Get down," Allissa said, her legs fanning out behind her.

"I, uh... yeah, sure." Leo took a deep breath and dropped so his neck was in the water.

"Now, hold on to the side like this." Allissa extended her arms and held on to the pool's edge. "We're just going to learn a basic stroke tonight."

5

"I've done alright with this, haven't I girl?" Andy raised his bottled beer towards the apartment's floor to ceiling windows. The towers of Manhattan sparkled across the waters of the Hudson River.

"Yes, you have," Emma agreed, standing next to him and raising her glass. Emma had never been to New York before, and she had to admit the view was beautiful. "Is that the —"

"Empire State Building, yeah." Andy pointed out the shining needle of the world-famous skyscraper. "When Michael said the place was going free for the holidays, I just knew we had to take it. We haven't had a holiday in... how long?"

"At least since Frankie was born," Emma said, taking a sip of prosecco. She twirled the glass's stem between her fingers. Emma and her friends would drink bottles and bottles of the stuff a few years ago. Now, she couldn't remember the last time she'd had even a single glass.

"Yeah, so well over two years." Andy tipped the remains of the beer into his mouth.

"Three years next month," Emma said absently.

Emma had always wanted to visit New York. The Big Apple. Emma glanced from the city across the water to her husband. Yet, now they were here, she didn't feel that excited. They were here on holiday, just the three of them. She should be excited.

Even though the flights had cost them all of their savings. Even though they now had very little money to spend while they were here. They were on holiday together as a family. Emma should be happy about that.

"It's not just that brother of yours who gets to go on holiday. We can have them too." Andy grabbed another beer from the fridge.

"They go away for work, really —"

"You call that work." Andy laughed out loud. "That Leo wouldn't know a day's work if it punched him in the face. We need the holiday more than him. We deserve it." Andy sauntered across the room and draped an arm around his wife. "And it's supposed to snow in a few days. How magical will that be? New York in the snow. It'll be like a fairy-tale."

Emma nodded but didn't reply. Andy put the fresh bottle of beer to his lips.

"The last year's been pretty tough, hasn't it?" he said after a long gulp.

Emma nodded again. That was an understatement. Since having Frankie, their lives had changed unrecognisably. More correctly, Emma's life had changed unrecognisably.

"But I told you we could make it work, though, didn't I?"

Emma stared out at the skyscrapers and took another deep swig of the prosecco. A boat slid regally up the river, its lights skipping across the water.

"You just needed to have a little faith in me, didn't you babes," Andy continued.

New York

"I've always had faith in you," Emma said. "That's why I said yes when you asked me to marry you."

"It wasn't for my looks then?" Andy grinned.

"Well, there was that too," Emma said, staring at her husband. Back in those days, Andy's hours in the gym made him taut and muscular. Now his hours on the sofa and the beer he drank gave him a soft paunch and a hard temper.

Emma forced a smile. They were in New York, and they were going to have a great time reconnecting with each other. For once, it even sounded as if Frankie had gone straight to sleep.

Emma drained her glass, then smiled and kissed her husband.

"But I wanted to spend my life with you, that's why I said yes." She hugged Andy and looked at the city over his shoulder.

The strobing lights of a helicopter skipped between the towers. A night-time helicopter tour of Manhattan — now that's something she'd really love to do. There was no way they'd be able to afford to, though. Just to have a night out in the smouldering city would probably cost too much.

"It's a beautiful place, isn't it?" Andy said.

"Yes," Emma replied, forcing a smile. "It really is."

"What've we got for dinner then?" Andy swigged the beer.

The pan on the stove rattled impatiently. Water hissed.

Gazing out at the skyline of the enchanting city, Emma had almost forgotten about dinner. She crossed to the kitchen and removed the lid from the pan.

"Pasta," Emma said. Steam billowed across the room.

"Nice." Andy sat at the table and rubbed his stomach. "As good as any Italian in this city, I reckon. You wouldn't come to New York for Italian food, anyway."

Emma's eyes flicked toward her husband. She didn't reply. Emma drained the pasta, stirred through the sauce and separated it into two bowls.

"Get us another beer while you're up," Andy said.

Emma took a bottle from the dwindling supply in the fridge, snapped it open and gave it to Andy. Then she carried their dinner across to the table and sat down herself.

"Na babe, best pasta in New York," Andy said, slurping the first mouthful. "I can tell you that for sure."

Emma didn't hear him. She stared through the windows at the glinting city beyond.

6

The city whispered and swished around him. To him, it seemed so obvious that he'd just killed someone. Yet, no one else had noticed. He'd worried they would sense it in his smile. See it in the flicker of his eyes, or the swing of his gait. But no. No one had noticed anything.

A group of women passed him on the sidewalk, giggling beneath colourful umbrellas. He watched them and resisted the urge to follow. The noise of the city had quietened with the coming night. The rumble of traffic was now just a few cars rustling past. A taxi's bright headlights sparkled from the wet asphalt. A wisp of steam snaked from a drain in the frigid night air.

A two-tone screech of sirens rose from the hubbub. The noise echoed fitfully from the surrounding buildings. The sirens neared. Blue and red lights flicked in nearby windows. A pair of police cars slid around the junction. Their tyres shrieked across the road, the drivers struggling to control their speed.

He turned to examine a restaurant's menu. The place

looked warm through steamy windows. It seemed to him, from the gloomy street and with the pressure of the blade in his sleeve, that the restaurant was another world entirely. A few diners glanced up as the police cars passed. Then they returned to their civil conversation and expensive meals. To them, the sirens were the rumble of a nightmare in another sleeper's head. An uncomfortable reminder of the city's dark side.

A large drip of rain caught him on the nose.

Didn't passing police cars make people wonder what had happened? Didn't they think about the grisly scene those cars were rushing to? What disaster? What act of violence they were going to discover?

He had wondered. He had always wondered.

The disturbance frustrated him. He'd picked the place carefully for two reasons, one of which was its solitude. He only needed fifteen minutes. Just fifteen minutes undisturbed. That's all his great-grandfather had been allowed, and look what he'd achieved. Genius — that's what.

He turned from the restaurant and walked on down the street. The events of the last few hours rode through his mind like a storm. He was a killer. He had done it.

He turned right at the intersection.

He hadn't been planning to kill again tonight. The night of the double murder wasn't for a while yet. But he'd only just begun to enjoy himself when his fun was curtailed.

The next site was close too, he knew, gripping the knife.

And there was no time like the present.

7
―――

"Sure, I been to Englan'," the diver yelled over the mini-bus's beefed-up stereo. Leo and Allissa squeezed into the front seats on their way to the island's weekly street party.

Leo glanced at the people behind them, all going to the party too.

The three women on the back seat cheered and clapped as a new tune began. Their colourful braids bounced to the beat of the song, which was something to do with being in a rum shop.

"Naaa, England's a cool place," the driver said, taking the corner with an ease that made Leo nervous.

Leo gripped the door. The thick alloy wheels of the suped-up bus screeched across the bumpy road. Allissa slid against Leo's shoulder. She wedged her feet into the footwell.

"When I say cool, I mean cold! Brrrrr!" the driver said, animating a shiver.

After Leo's first swimming lesson, they'd gone back to their rooms and got changed. Then they'd enjoyed a couple of beers in one of the hotel's bars, before joining the group waiting for the bus to the street party.

"I remember getting off the plane when I first arrived in Englan'," the driver said, accelerating down a straight stretch on the narrow road. "I went for a smoke outside the airport. I pulled on the cigarette proper deep, hadn't had one in hours. Then, when I breathed out, the smoke just didn't stop! I was like, how big are these lungs?"

The tune changed, and the bus erupted into whoops and cheers. The driver battered the steering wheel to the beat. The bus swayed to the rhythm.

Leo's knuckles whitened on the door handle. He was glad they'd sunk a couple of beers before leaving. The journey would have been fear-inducing if he were stone-cold sober.

Leo and Allissa hadn't been out together for a long time. Leo couldn't actually remember the last time — Hong Kong, maybe. So, when they'd heard about the weekly street party, both were keen to attend. A night of drinking, relaxation and — if Allissa got her way — dancing.

"Dis street party is legendary." The driver grinned at them in the rear-view mirror. The bus slowed as they approached the centre of town. "It's been going years. You never seen a party like we have on this island."

"What sort of music do they play?" Allissa asked.

"Mmmmm, they play the best type." The driver pointed at the stereo. He thumbed a button, and another tune played. The passengers in the back of the bus cheered, and the driver cranked the volume to an ear-splitting level.

"The music that makes you wanna," shouted the woman sat behind Allissa. "You and your boyfriend gonna love it!" She put her hand on Allissa's shoulder.

"We're not —" Leo started.

"Loosen him up a bit, you know what I mean? Where ya from?" the woman asked Allissa.

"England," Allissa explained.

"So cold."

The driver pulled over, the door slid open and the passengers tumbled out.

"Down there on the right," the driver yelled, pointing. Passengers passed money through the driver's open window and wandered away, singing and dancing, towards the party.

"You can't miss it," the driver shouted. "Make sure you stay 'till the end... that's when they play the best music."

8
―――

"Open another bottle, babe. We're on holiday."

"I'm not sure I should. I mean, what if Frankie —"

"Nonsense. Let me. I'll do it for you." Andy hoisted himself from the sleek, red leather sofa and lumbered across the open-plan living room. "We're on holiday, and if my wife wants another glass of prosecco, then that's what she'll have."

Emma slotted the plates into the dishwasher, dried her hands and crossed to the sofa.

"Okay, if you're sure." Emma smiled at Andy and looked longingly at the city beyond the window.

Emma had only met Andy's older brother Michael at their wedding and had no idea what he did for a living. Whatever it was, he clearly made a lot of money. An apartment like this with a view over Manhattan definitely didn't come cheap.

Andy cracked open the bottle. Prosecco streamed to the floor. "That's the way to do it. You need a bit to fizz up like that, otherwise you've not done it right. Here you go," he said as he filled Emma's glass. Again, it fizzed over the top. He returned the bottle to the fridge, grabbed himself another beer and slouched across to the sofa.

"It's like that time we were staying... where was it we were staying? You know, when we'd first met?" Andy slumped his arm around Emma's shoulders.

She took a sip of the prosecco, which had now simmered down to a third of the glass. "Manchester?".

"Yeah, that was it. That was a great weekend, wasn't it?"

"Yes, it was,"

Six months after they'd met, Andy had surprised Emma with a weekend away. It had been lovely, but was the only example of such a gesture in their entire relationship.

"You know," Andy said, looking around, "we could have a place like this one day. If we wanted."

"Really? This would cost loads, wouldn't it?"

"Just a couple of mill." Andy stifled a hiccup. "When my business takes off, we'll get something like this, no problem. We've had a good year so far, got some exciting contracts. I reckon things are going in the right direction."

Emma had seen the accounts. She knew that Andy's small-scale construction business was a fair way from making a million.

"It's not all about the money though." Emma turned to face her husband.

"Well, it sort of is, isn't it? It's money that got us here, and money pays for our house and food. I'd like to hear you say that if our accounts ran dry." Andy gulped his beer.

Emma thought of the well-paid job she'd given up when Frankie was born. Andy had said, "No son of mine will be sent away to some day-care place. A mum's job is to look after him." It was an attitude which, despite all Emma's protests, her research into child development, and the financial benefits of keeping her salary, Andy just wouldn't drop. Emma had conceded in the end, and spent the last three years almost single-handedly raising their son.

"Just you watch, babe," Andy grumbled, "I've got a few big contracts coming in, and they'll see us right."

The problem was, Andy had been saying that for years, leaving them struggling and living paycheque to paycheque in the meantime.

Emma took a fortifying sip of the prosecco and sat up straight. They needed to have this conversation. She wasn't putting it off any longer.

9

Leo and Allissa heard the rumbling bass the moment they stepped from the bus. People wandered towards the sound in droves. Hips draped in red, yellow and green swayed to the beat. Leo felt the excitement of the party take hold.

The combined smells of barbecued meat, charcoal and the sweet citrus of rum punch were as heady as the music. Speakers stacked on the back of a truck grunted and groaned. Even from behind the crowd of up-stretched arms, Leo felt the bassline.

"Rum punch, you wan' rum punch?" shouted a large woman from behind a table. The makeshift bar glowed beneath festoons of hanging bulbs.

"Sure," Allissa said, grinning, "we'll take two. Thanks."

"No problem, miss, two of da best punches comin' up."

Ice snapped as the woman filled two plastic cups with pink liquid. Leo accepted one and took a big gulp. It was sweet and strong.

The deep thumping beat of a hip-hop tune faded, and the vibrant sound of Caribbean soca pounded across the street. The crowd whooped and hollered. A group of women rushed past Leo. One of them took Allissa by the arm and led her into the crowd. Allissa moved effortlessly to the beat. Light danced across her wide smile.

Leo shook his head, raised his hands in surrender, and moved into the dancing throng.

Rum flowed. Gyrating bodies with upstretched arms swarmed and stomped. The music was like nothing Leo had heard before. The deep thumping bass embodied the heat, the rum, the smiling people and the island.

Leo finished his third or fourth rum punch and gazed at the crowd. The St Lucians, of which Allissa was now an honorary member, twisted naturally to the beat. Leo, by comparison, moved awkwardly and out of time.

"Let's get a drink," Allissa shouted over the music. She pointed at their empty plastic cups in Leo's hands. Holding an empty cup impeded Allissa's instinctive dance moves, Leo supposed.

"Alright," Leo yelled back and followed Allissa through the crowd.

"That was great!" Allissa turned to look at Leo as the music quietened. "Even got you dancing."

Allissa took their empty cups and pushed towards one of the rum stalls.

Leo needed to jump back into that cold pool again — even without the ability to swim.

"This is wicked, isn't it?" came an English-accented voice from behind him. Leo turned and saw a young man, tanned, and with all the clichés of a backpacker. A beaded bracelet hung from one wrist and a leather one on the other.

"Yeah, so good," Leo shouted back.

"I'm Matt." The man held out a hand. "This is Tess, my

wife." He pointed to a pretty, petite, and equally tanned woman beside him.

"It's our honeymoon," Tess said, leaning to kiss Leo on the cheek. "You're here with your..." Tess pointed at Allissa, approaching with the drinks.

"This is Allissa," Leo said.

"It was a small ceremony," Tess said when Allissa asked about their wedding.

"Not small enough," Matt whispered to Leo.

The pair's honeymoon was a six-month trip, starting in the Caribbean, before travelling on through Central and South America.

Leo listened as Tess talked about their trip and thought of a woman he once knew. A woman who had changed his life. Mya. If it hadn't been for Mya disappearing on their own trip around the world all those years ago, he would have never met Allissa.

"Shots!" Matt shouted, snapping Leo from his memories. "We're celebrating tonight, so we definitely need shots."

"Yes!" Allissa shouted back.

"Sure," Leo said through a hazy smile. "I'll get them in."

10

"There's something I want to talk to you about," Emma said, clasping the stem of the glass tightly between her hands. "Remember Danielle, the lady I used to work with?"

"Yeah," Andy grumbled angrily.

"Well, she's setting up a marketing agency, and she wants me to head up some accounts. She's been asking for a while, but last week she made me an offer. A really good offer."

Andy's mouth chewed over unsaid words. His eyes narrowed.

"How much?" he finally said.

The figure made Andy's face pale. It was almost three times what Andy's firm made in a year.

"I... I..." Andy fumbled the words, then got to his feet and paced across the kitchen.

"How long've you been going behind my back and arranging shit like this?" He turned to Emma, his eyes fierce.

"I haven't arranged anything," Emma said calmly. "Danielle wants me to work there. She contacted me. I said no at first, but I think this offer is good... too good to refuse. We could start paying off some debts and have regular holidays."

"What're we doing now?" Andy shouted. "This is a fucking holiday, isn't it?"

Emma didn't reply.

"I'm providing you with holidays. Are you that selfish?" Andy's shoulders tensed and his knuckles whitened around the bottle. "Let me get this right." Andy's voice dropped to a malevolent whisper. "I'm out there, day and night, busting my balls to provide for this family, and all the while you're scheming of ways you think you can do it better?"

"No, it's not like that," Emma said. "It's not like that at all. Both parents in most families work. That's normal. Plus, you didn't even let me finish. Danielle says I could work from home whenever I wanted and be totally flexible with my hours. We could look after Frankie together."

"No way," Andy said. His fist crashed to the kitchen counter. "Look at this place. This is what I've provided for you and Frankie. Look out there!"

Andy crossed the room, pulled Emma up from the sofa and turned her towards the window.

"This is what I provide for you, and you think you can do better?"

Andy's fingers dug into Emma's skin. She winced at the pain.

"Let go. You're hurting me. Let go!"

Andy let Emma go and stormed over to the fridge. He downed the rest of his beer and grabbed another. "I've been working day and night for this family," Andy reiterated drunkenly, "and you want to out do me like that." He snapped his fingers.

"It's not about outdoing you," Emma said, straining to

keep her voice calm. This conversation needed to happen. "I want to go back to work. Not just because of the money, but because I'm good at it."

"You're good at being a mum. That's your job now."

"Yes, and I love being a mum. But I need more conversation than listening to Frankie burble on all day." Andy paced around the room. "I know you've been working hard. If I worked too, you wouldn't have to work quite so much. You could go out with your friends, go to the gym again, we could go on more holidays."

"We're here, aren't we?" Andy repeated.

"We are," Emma whispered, "but we can't even afford to go for a meal out. It's hardly a holiday if we can't leave the apartment."

A bottle smashed against the wall. Emma leapt from her seat. Andy's eyes focused on her.

"That's what it's all about, is it? Living the high life, drinking cocktails and wearing posh clothes —"

"I'm not saying —"

"I know exactly what you're saying."

Andy stalked towards Emma. His fists, thick white balls.

"Alright, alright," she said, her hands outstretched in surrender. "Don't worry about it, we'll just —"

11

Children fear the shadows. He remembered being a child and fearing the shadows himself. Or rather, being a child and fearing what might lurk unseen in those shadows.

But adults weren't afraid. They'd checked enough shadows for goblins or monsters that now they just assumed there was nothing there. They didn't even bother to look anymore.

He smiled. It was funny, he thought as he nestled in the shadowy passage beside Hanbury's clothes shop. He had chosen Hanbury's on purpose. Expensive clothes shone beneath bright lights in the shop's window, right next to the place which would, with a bit of luck, be the scene of his second victim's demise.

He looked at the dark fabric of his raincoat. The shadow submerged him. Right here, he looked like nothing. An exterminating angel. Ready to strike. An oil slick heading for an untouched beach. A black hole in a cluster of stars. Soon he would drag her into his nothingness.

The rain intensified. He narrowed his eyes. It would have been like this in London all those years ago.

This was the best way to kill.

The voice in his head sounded like an expert now. He was an expert—he was a killer. This was the best way to kill because, on the face of it, he had no reason to kill these women. If you thought about it logically, as people often did, he didn't even know them. There was no link whatsoever. He'd watched enough documentaries and read enough true crime stories to know that suspicion automatically fell on the victim's friends. Everyone's closet was full of skeletons, and some skeletons were worth killing for.

His motivations were different, though. The victims themselves weren't important. They were like an artist's paint or a sculptor's marble. The means to an end. An end, which would make them all worthwhile.

A car passed. Its tyres hissed against the wet tarmac. He ducked further into the shadow to avoid the glare. The brake lights flickered on, bathing the street in a violent red. The door clunked open.

"Thanks for nothing," came an aggressive female voice. "I said stop three times back there. If you were paying attention —"

He couldn't hear the driver's response.

"No, forget it. I'm not paying you to go around again. Next time just listen, alright?"

His fingers closed around the knife.

"You can absolutely forget about the tip. I want that change."

The taxi sloshed away. This was it.

12

"Honestly, it's fine," Emma said, her eyes darting from the smashed bottle on the floor to her approaching husband. "I'll tell Danielle that family comes first, and I need to be there for you and Frankie."

Andy paused. His jaw clenched.

"Let me get you another drink, and we'll enjoy the evening. I shouldn't have said anything." Emma jumped to her feet and darted to the kitchen.

Andy grumbled something inaudible. His shoulders slumped.

"You've finished all the beers," Emma said, turning from the fridge. She opened Michael's spirit cupboard. "Sit down. I'll make you something from here. Forget I said anything, please."

Andy sunk into the sofa. He fumed with anger.

Emma poured a generous measure of whiskey into a glass and returned to the couch.

"I know how hard you're working," she said again, sitting

beside Andy. "I didn't mean to upset you. I'm sorry about that."

Andy accepted the glass and drank half of it straight away.

"It's just that I... I..." he mumbled. "I want you and Frankie to have... have the best things. You deserve that."

"And we do," Emma said.

Andy's thick hand slithered onto Emma's knee.

"You enjoy your drink, and I'll clean up this glass," Emma said. "I'd hate Frankie to see it or for it to stain."

Emma stood and Andy's hand dropped to the leather. He gazed at his wife through unfocused eyes, then lifted the whiskey to his lips and downed it in one.

Emma stepped into the hallway and took a deep breath. She held it for a few seconds. Her heart thumped. Her reflection in the mirror was pale.

Was this really her life now? Was she now nothing more than a servant to her husband and son?

Emma had loved her life before Frankie was born. She had lots of friends and a busy social calendar. Now she couldn't remember the last time she'd left the house. Andy met everything she suggested with scorn. It was either too expensive, or not the sort of thing he wanted his wife and son to be doing. She was trapped.

Emma fetched the dustpan and brush from the closet and returned to the front room.

Andy lay on the sofa, his head tilted back, his mouth gaping, snoring loudly. His glass lay sideways on the floor.

Emma knelt down and swept up the broken glass, then got to her feet. Manhattan's skyline glimmered invitingly through the window.

There was a world of opportunity. A world of opportunity, all of which Emma was missing out on, and all because of Andy. She turned and looked at him. A wave of anger bubbled through her. He was so stubborn and dominating. If he just accepted that he couldn't do everything himself, then they could make this work. But right now — tears welled from her eyes — right now she just couldn't carry on.

She couldn't do this. She needed to go.

Emma grabbed her bag as tears streamed across her face. Although they'd spent most of their savings on the flights over here, Emma still had a personal account, which Andy didn't know about. It wasn't much, but there should be enough for her and Frankie to stay in a hotel for a few days.

Emma stuffed some of Frankie's clothes into the bag and booked a taxi. She hadn't taken everything, just enough for the next few days. She lifted Frankie from his bed and pulled his coat around him. There was no need to wake him up.

Emma stepped from the building with Frankie in one arm and her bag in the other. Her taxi waited at the kerb. The driver got out and helped her with the case.

"Take me to a hotel in Manhattan, somewhere near Central Park," Emma whispered, sliding into the back.

"Sure thing," the driver said. "I know just the place."

Emma looked up at the building as the taxi pulled away. Things were going to change. Emma knew that, one way or another, things were going to change.

13

"Four sambucas," Matt said, showing the number with his fingers. "So how long have you and Allissa..." he asked Leo.

"We're... urrm..." Leo said, glancing over at Allissa, now deep in conversation with Tess. "About two years."

"Ahh cool, that's great. How d'you meet?"

Leo thought about his response for a moment. "I worked for her dad for a while," he said.

"Nice. What did the old man think of that?"

"He wasn't best pleased at first," Leo said, remembering the events through which he'd met Allissa in Kathmandu. "I think he's used to it now though."

Despite Leo's efforts to pay, Matt handed a note to the barman. They took two shots each and made their way back to Allissa and Tess.

Music throbbed from the speakers. The crowd became more fevered with each tune the DJ dropped.

"To holidays," Matt said, raising his glass.

The others raised their glasses together before downing the shots.

"Right, let's dance," Allissa shouted, beckoning them towards the twirling crowd, her hips swinging to the beat.

14

Andy opened his eyes slowly. "Emma?" He blinked and rubbed a hand across his face.

The apartment was dark. "What the —"

He remembered the conversation with Emma. The row about her returning to work. The hazy, drink-fuelled rage he'd felt.

"Oh shit," he muttered.

Andy struggled to his feet. The room spun around him. His back and neck ached.

Emma had probably gone to bed without him. He needed to apologise. Andy had the distinct feeling he'd done something terrible. He examined the room but couldn't see any evidence of his misdeeds. There weren't even any empty glasses in the kitchen. The city shone through the window.

It was okay to have a couple of drinks at the start of the holiday, wasn't it? Of course it was. A few drinks on holiday was normal. He padded through to the bedroom and snapped on the light.

"Hey Em, I'm sorry," he said. "I shouldn't have —"

The blankets lay folded, just as they were when they'd arrived. The bed was empty.

"Emma?" Andy muttered. Maybe he'd pissed her off so much she was sleeping in another room.

He wandered down the corridor and pushed open the door to the spare room.

"Emma," he mumbled. "I'm —"

The spare room was empty too.

She must be sleeping in Frankie's room. Andy switched on the light and recognised the normal trimmings of a young boy's room. The room belonged to his nephew. Three teddy bears considered him through vacant eyes. Colourful animals covered the walls.

Andy's sense of foreboding grew. He crossed to the bed. This bed was empty too.

He rushed back to the master bedroom. His suitcase lay alone beside the bed. Emma's case had gone.

15

He stood up and looked down at the body. Her neck was twisted at a strange angle. One arm extended upwards, the other bent beneath her.

He gripped the knife in his right hand. A trickle of blood dripped from the tip and puddled on the concrete.

He couldn't help but feel disappointed. This contorted body just wasn't as perfect as the first one. Knife slashes crisscrossed her face, and he'd stabbed her three times in the stomach. She would never look as radiant as his first. He imagined the pearly-white skin lying naked in the gloom.

This one was already disfigured. Disfigured, because she couldn't die as he needed her too. She just had to fight back, didn't she. *Bitch!*

Maybe he'd got lucky with the first one. There was something special there. He'd felt her life fading peacefully as blood oozed from her neck. It was spiritual. Godlike. That was the feeling he'd craved. Heavenly. He'd watched her eyes flutter for the last time as she slid from this life and into the next.

The result was the same, though, he supposed — a

crumpled body in an alleyway. Although, this one looked far from heavenly. There wasn't time to complain. There wasn't time for anything.

He bent over and cut open her bright yellow coat. He wanted to get that out of sight as soon as possible. Bright colours would show up in the dark passageway. He pulled the coat out from beneath her and threw it behind a dumpster.

He straightened her arms. She looked better with her arms by her sides.

He cut off her blood soaked jumper and threw it to one side. Three ferocious stab wounds gazed up from her stomach. He hadn't planned to stab her, but he'd needed to make the noise stop. He couldn't have her screaming and shouting like that.

He cut off her top and pulled it from her torso. She wasn't as shapely as the last one either. Her body was wider, and sagged in places where the other's had been pert and perfect. He closed his eyes and pictured the previous body.

He snarled and tightened his grip on the knife.

It didn't really matter though, he thought. He wouldn't let it matter. She's made the ultimate sacrifice for him — that's all that mattered.

He pulled up the left sleeve of his raincoat and looked at the bracelet. It wasn't what she looked like to start with — that wasn't the point. It was what he did with them that made the difference. He lifted the bracelet to his lips and kissed it.

"This is for you," he whispered. "It's all in honour of you."

16

Andy's anger rose as he walked back into the living room. *He* had arranged this holiday. It had been *his* idea to come in the first place, and they were staying in *his* brother's apartment.

Yes, Emma had booked the flights and stuff like that — the boring and easy stuff — but the entire thing was his idea. She couldn't just go off and have a better time on her own. That wasn't how it worked.

Andy's eyes alighted on a bottle of whiskey on the kitchen counter. A pang of recognition chimed somewhere — had he been drinking this too? He picked it up and examined the logo. It looked expensive. He twisted off the top and took a sip. It tasted good.

That was the thing about Michael — he had good taste. Andy grew up seeing his older brother with expensive things, whether it was a top of the range car, the latest phone, or designer clothes. Michael could always afford it with his well-paid job in pharmaceuticals. Money had never been a problem for him.

Andy took another swig of the whisky. It just wasn't fair.

Andy's wife, Maria, stayed at home to be a mum, too. Why did Emma make such a fuss over it?

It wasn't like he was asking something outrageous of her. He just wanted her to stay at home and look after their son. Her son!

Andy quelled his anger with another swig of the whiskey and stepped across to the window. New York's skyline smouldered across the river.

What was it Emma had said? "It's hardly a holiday if we can't leave the apartment."

His rage spiked again. Emma wasn't going out and having a great time while he stayed at home. No fucking way. Andy remembered he didn't have any money, and again thought about his brother. His eyebrows knotted in concentration. Michael would definitely keep some cash in the apartment. The guy was minted.

He strode back over to the kitchen and rummaged through the drawers and cupboards. He shoved cutlery, crockery and saucepans aside. Nothing. He had another drink then stalked over to a side table. He searched through each of the drawers. Nothing.

He swayed blindly through to the bedroom with the bottle still in his hand. He tore open the wardrobe, yanked clothes from the rail and tossed them on the floor. Then he emptied each of the drawers in the dressing table onto the floor. Not a thing. He staggered over to another chest of drawers and dumped the contents of the bottom two drawers onto the bed. A scowl etched the sides of his mouth. Andy turned back to the chest of drawers, slid open the top drawer and looked inside. His face then contorted into a grin. Inside, amongst a load of papers, was a gold watch, a few rings, a crisp bundle of notes and a set of car keys.

"I knew you'd come through for me, Michael," Andy whispered.

He slid the notes into his pocket and examined the watch. It looked expensive. Andy then picked up the car keys. Seeing a picture of Michael's Porsche online had made Andy resent his seven-year-old Honda Civic. Andy glanced at the keys in his sweaty palm and smirked.

He turned and looked at himself in the mirror. *I can't go out like this, though. No way.* He stared at the pile of clothes on the bed. Even in a crumpled heap, they looked well-cut and expensive. He selected a shirt, trousers and a jacket, then changed quickly and stood in front of the mirror. He stashed the money in his pocket, grabbed the bottle of whiskey and headed for the door.

The lights in the underground car park snapped on as Andy stepped from the lift. He pressed the key and the lights of a red Porsche Boxster flashed.

Andy slid into the driver's seat and put the bottle beside him. He pressed the start button, and he smiled as the Porsche grumbled to life. The twin exhaust's throaty thump echoed through the car park. He pumped the accelerator. The car's grumble became a roar. Andy programmed the sat nav to take him to Manhattan. That's where the parties would be. Directions filled the screen. Andy pulled on his seatbelt and took another swig of the whiskey. Then, snapping the car into drive, he slid the Porsche out of the car park.

"New York, are you ready?"

17

"How good was that?" Allissa said. "We even got you dancing too."

"Yeah, it was fun," Leo agreed as he rolled down the taxi window. Music drifted through the still night air as they drew away from the centre of the town.

"Does this happen every week?" Allissa asked the driver.

"Yeah, every week. The island is known for it. Everyone goes." He grinned at Leo and Allissa in the rear-view mirror.

Leo tasted the sticky sweetness of the shots on his tongue. They'd drunk a lot. Allissa beamed drunkenly beside him.

"Why weren't you there then?" Allissa asked. "Don't you like the party?"

"Oh, I like the party alright," the man said. "I like the party too much. Because of the party, I got three baby mamas to support now."

"I see," Allissa said. "Is one of them your girlfriend?"

"Na,"— the driver laughed — "not yet, anyway. My girlfriend hasn't got children yet. Maybe one day."

"Yeah, that must be expensive. How old are the children?"

Leo listened to the conversation as the car picked up speed. They were out of the town now, and the darkened landscape streamed past the windows. Getting away from work for a while was great. The last few weeks had been non-stop. In fact, it had been non-stop since he and Allissa had first met.

"Let me get this right," Allissa said, eyebrows knitted in concentration, "as soon as this girlfriend is a baby mama, you'll get yourself a different girlfriend?"

The driver nodded.

"It's just going to get even more expensive then, isn't it?"

"Yeah, so I'll just have to work even more. Here you go," he said, stopping alongside the resort's entrance.

Allissa and Leo thanked the man and stepped out into the night. Insects hummed and zinged. The bars and restaurants now sat empty and dark. A bed of jewels swayed across the surface of the murky pool. Wind hissed through the palm trees, and the sea purred against the sand.

"It looks like we've got the place to ourselves," Leo said.

"This way," Allissa said, leading him down to the beach. "Midnight swimming lesson?" She broke into a run towards the purring waves.

"Hell no," Leo said. "That's really dangerous, don't go in there."

Leo was suddenly alert. His heart pounded, and his breathing quickened. He gazed into the gloom, but couldn't see any further than a few feet in front of him.

"Allissa, don't —"

"Oh, come on," she said, appearing by his side. "What sort of reckless idiot do you think I am? This is beautiful, though." She dropped to the sand and stretched out her legs. The moon hung ripe and low above the ocean.

Leo sat beside her and let the wrestling ocean and the distant mumble of the jungle absorb him. Many years ago, in therapy for his anxiety, Leo had started the practice of concentrating on the surrounding sounds. It was a habit which had stuck, and now, through his drink-fogged mind, Leo listened closely to it all.

"Remember that afternoon in Kathmandu, when you turned up at guesthouse pretending to be my brother?" Allissa asked.

"Of course," Leo replied.

"Did you ever think it would end up like this? Even for a moment."

"Not in a million years. Absolutely no way. It's like a film."

"It's been good fun," Allissa said.

"It's been dangerous."

"Yes, it has been dangerous too, that's true," she agreed, laughing. "But that's the life we've chosen, I suppose." Her voice sounded wistful. She looked up at the blanket of stars, then glanced at Leo on the sand beside her.

"If it were a film, who do you think would play you?" Allissa asked.

Leo mumbled.

Allissa looked out at the inky black ocean.

"Do you think we'll still be doing stuff like this next year?" Allissa asked.

Leo didn't answer.

"I would like to be," Allissa said, her words flowing easily. "I think... If you would?"

Then she heard it. To start with, it was only faint. Then it came again, louder this time.

Leo was snoring.

"Oi," Allissa shouted, jabbing Leo in the ribs.

"What? Hey... sorry, what?" Leo managed. "What did you say? Sorry, was just resting my eyes?"

"Bollocks you were." Allissa smiled, rose to her feet, and pulled Leo toward their separate rooms. "It's past your bedtime, grandad."

18

Andy drove slowly through Hoboken's wide streets. It was late and the night was quiet. He stopped at a traffic light. The Porsche's engine grumbled, begging for speed.

A pair of women walked along the street, probably on their way home from a bar. Andy lowered the window and smiled. Then, as the lights changed, he floored the accelerator. The Porsche flew ahead. Andy pushed the car harder. His teeth bared with exhilaration.

He followed the sat nav's directions and turned right onto the turnpike for the Lincoln Tunnel. Manhattan's skyline flashed across the river. That's where he was going.

"New York, baby!" he shouted through the car's open window.

Tyres screeched across the asphalt as he descended towards the Lincoln Tunnel. Andy slowed for the barrier which popped up as the car approached. The mouth of the tunnel beckoned him on. Andy didn't need the encouragement.

He lowered both windows to hear the engine and crushed the accelerator. The Porsche growled on. The engine sang, and the needle flickered into the red. The car wanted more.

Through bloodshot eyes, Andy watched the car devour the strip of tarmac. The row of lights on the tunnel's ceiling strobed passed. He overtook a bus lumbering down the inside lane.

The speedometer crept skyward. Andy didn't notice. He didn't care.

One wrong nudge of the wheel here and he'd smash into the wall.

Ahead, the tunnel curved to the right. Andy pushed harder into the corner. A warning sign flashed by. Andy didn't see it. Andy didn't care.

The roar of the Porsche's engine reverberated from the tunnel's bare walls.

Andy narrowed his eyes. The needle crept past one-hundred and ten.

Was that miles-per-hour?

Andy padded the brake. The corner continued. Tyres screeched across the asphalt. The car slid into the outside lane. That was okay — the tunnel was empty. The wall flashed by just inches away.

The sound of screaming tyres and roaring engines thronged from wall to road and back again.

Andy gritted his teeth. His thick hands blanched on the wheel. He dabbed the brake, and the speedometer dipped below one-hundred. The car slid nearer the outside wall. Andy pushed the brake as hard as he dared. Too much would send the car into a skid. Then he'd have no control.

Andy's jaw pulsed with tension and his bloodshot eyes

widened on the tunnel ahead. He tapped the brake harder this time. His speed dropped, and the Porsche gained some traction. Another warning sign flashed past.

Time slowed. Andy pushed everything he could into the car and the corner. His muscles strained. He held his breath.

A large maintenance truck, surrounded by flashing lights and cones, crept along the left-hand lane. Andy's eyes widened. His body jarred into position.

The Porsche slid uncontrollably towards the truck. Cones skittered around the car. One spun over the windscreen, bouncing from the glass with a dull thunk.

Andy squeezed the brake and twisted the wheel harder. Each bump of the tarmac pulsated through his tensed shoulders.

The Porsche didn't want to move. It barrelled onwards towards the truck.

Late night road workers ran for cover.

There was no time to think.

Andy's drunken synapses fired. His heart thumped. He glanced at the speedometer. Ninety.

He had two choices. The solid rear of the truck, or the welcoming wall of the tunnel.

Andy made his choice. He spun the wheel.

Nothing happened at first.

He gripped the wheel harder and yanked further.

The tyres howled. The Porsche whipped to the right. The tunnel spun before his eyes.

Everything slowed for a moment.

The Porsche crunched against the side of the tunnel. The airbag detonated, blocking Andy's view. The car spun, then rolled, then bumped. Metal crunched and glass shattered. Tyres thumped and howled against the road. Andy bounced forwards into the airbag, then back into the seat, then forward again. He didn't know which direction he was travelling. The car screeched and skipped for fifty meters before jarring to a stop.

Silence descended. Still, dark and thick.

19

Emma's resolve waned when she awoke to Frankie crying in their hotel room. The hotel had cost more than she'd imagined. It was cramped, noisy, and the thought of spending more than a few hours here with a three-year-old filled her with regret.

She thought of Michael's spacious apartment across the river, crammed with modern conveniences and more toys than Frankie would ever need. She could just go back to Andy now, enjoy the holiday, and talk about it all when they got home. Maybe, if they could just have a good holiday, then they could even find a way to make it work between them.

After a cup of average coffee and an eye-wateringly expensive room-service breakfast, she made her decision. She grabbed her suitcase and handed back the room key in reception with a flush of embarrassment.

Dragging her suitcase towards the bus stop, Emma looked at the towering buildings around her. Frankie stopped to pick up a crushed tin can from the gutter. Emma longed to explore the city, but couldn't do it like this. Not with a toddler in tow.

An hour later, Emma stepped from the lift and paused at the door of the apartment. What if Andy never changed? He might continue to get drunk, and worse, become violent towards her. Could she cope with that?

He'd been close last night to hitting her, Emma could tell.

Emma stood at the door, drew in a deep breath and looked down at Frankie. They would make it work for now — for the holiday. She could do that. They needed to do that.

"We're home," Emma called as she opened the door.

There was no reply.

A weird feeling of doubt rose in Emma's throat. She swallowed it down and forced a smile.

Frankie wiggled and groaned in her arms. He didn't like being carried.

"Andy?" she called out again.

Maybe he was still asleep. It was probably best to leave him to it.

Emma walked into the lounge and put Frankie on the floor. The room looked as it had the night before. Frankie examined the pile of his cousin's toys.

Emma wandered over to the apartment's top-spec kitchen. Everything was in its place. She wasn't sure what she might come back to, but a tidy apartment wasn't it. There was no sign that anyone was even here.

Emma's face twisted into a scowl. Her sense of disquiet rose.

Emma's head thumped. She'd drunk a few glasses of wine last night. She wasn't used to that anymore.

She slid open the kitchen drawers and found a pack of

painkillers. She popped two pills onto the counter, filled a glass with water, and swallowed them. Then she set about making coffee. A strong one. Probably the first of many.

Michael and Maria had the Rolls Royce of all coffee machines. Emma had suggested to Andy they buy one when they moved to their new house.

"All that just for a drink," Andy had replied.

Emma knew that if the machine produced vodka, then Andy would have bought it in a second. Emma slid a mug beneath the dual spouts. The machine studiously ground and hissed. The smell of roasted coffee beans filled the room. The machine finished its work with a crescendo of wheezing steam. Emma switched it off and took her cup over to the sofa. She dropped into the chair, gazed at the skyline of New York against the deep blue sky, and took a long sip of the bitter, revitalising liquid.

How had her life become this complicated?

All she wanted was a simple family life. She just wanted to get married and have children. How complicated was that?

Last night had been one of their worst arguments yet. Although, if she were being honest, things hadn't been great since Frankie's birth. Maybe even before. Emma had wanted their marriage to work so much. She'd tried everything she could to make him happy.

Their house was everything Emma thought she'd need to live *'happily ever after'*. But it wasn't everything she needed. She knew that now. That had become obvious. If things didn't change, if they didn't get better, Emma knew they'd have to separate. She couldn't carry on like this.

Emma didn't want them to break up. The prospect of being a single mother was terrifying. But she couldn't live like this. Not for much longer, anyway.

Maybe she should wait until Frankie was a little older? Then, he'd be at school, and Emma could make more use of her time. She could go back to work. She loved her job. Sure, it was only "selling stuff," as Andy had crowed in one of their arguments, but she enjoyed it.

And it wasn't *only* selling stuff, anyway — unless you considered spending over twenty million quid a year for some of the country's biggest retailers just "selling stuff".

Emma had suggested that Andy give up his job to look after Frankie. They could afford to live comfortably on her salary. It was more than Andy earned, anyway.

"Your job now is to look after Frankie," he'd said.

"We'll get a childminder or take him to a nursery, like most children," Emma replied.

"No child of mine is going to…"

Emma gave up. There was no point arguing with him. Knowing the statistics on the benefits of children attending pre-school was pointless if Andy wasn't listening.

Was it any surprise that their love had dried up when all they fed it was resentment?

The door entry system buzzed.

"Maybe that's daddy," Emma said to Frankie, who wasn't paying any attention. "I bet the silly man's gone out and forgotten his key."

She put the coffee down and walked across to the door. The apartment had one of those video entry systems which remotely gave people access. Emma hadn't used it before. She picked up the receiver and the small screen flickered to life.

"Hello?"

"It's the Hoboken Police Department," came the voice down the line. "You're going to have to let us in."

20

Nausea welled in Emma's stomach as she opened the apartment door. A churning, bubbling, acidic torrent rose in her throat. She leaned against the wall and tried to control it.

The lift doors slid open, and two police officers stepped out. One was a stocky man with tightly curled hair, the other an Asian woman.

"Good morning." The female officer spoke first. "We're looking for a Michael Harris, is he here?"

Emma's mouth opened, but no words came out. Her sense of sickness soared.

"Come in, come in." Emma beckoned desperately. "I'm just –" She bent double and covered her mouth with her hands. She swayed into the bathroom as the officers shut the door behind them.

"I'm sorry," Emma said when she emerged two minutes later. "I've not been feeling well all morning. Michael's not here, no. He's my brother-in-law. My husband and I are house-sitting for him." Emma looked anxiously from one officer to the other. Although the sick feeling had bubbled away, tension now knotted her chest.

"How long have they been away, Mrs...?"

"Emma, please. They went three days ago, and we arrived yesterday."

Frankie stared up from the endless task of spreading toys around the room, a toy car gripped in each hand.

"Have either of you used his car during the time you've been here?" The male officer glanced at a notepad. "A red Porsche Boxster."

"No, we haven't. We only arrived yesterday afternoon and haven't been out since. Why?"

"Mr Harris's car was involved in an incident last night, and we're trying to understand what happened."

"What?" Emma gasped. "That's not possible." The tension knotted harder across her chest. "It must have been stolen or something. Did anyone see the person driving it?"

"No, the car was empty by the time we arrived."

Emma shook her head and looked from the police officers to a spot on the floor. "It must have been stolen or something. We've not used it." She looked up. Clouds hung malevolently over the city through the window. "I didn't even know Michael had a car."

Frankie bashed a toy car against the floor and shrieked. Emma and the police officers glanced at him.

"How old is your son?"

"He's three next week," Emma said, smiling at the familiar conversation. "He's a real terror."

"Are we able to speak with your husband too? Just to see if he noticed anything," the male officer said.

"Of course," Emma said. "I'll go and wake him. We had a long flight yesterday."

Emma turned and walked towards the bedroom. She

crossed the hall and pushed open the bedroom door. Then she gasped. She fell against the wall for support.

"Mrs Harris, are you okay?" The police officers rushed after her. Emma didn't hear. All she could see was the state of the bedroom. Drawers empty, clothes pulled from the wardrobe, and Andy's suitcase upturned on the floor. In the centre of the chaos, the bed was empty.

The officers appeared at Emma's side.

"Is this the bedroom Mr Harris was supposed to be staying in?"

Emma nodded.

"Where did you stay?"

Between gasps, Emma explained about the argument and her night in the hotel.

"I'll check the other rooms," the female officer said, heading for the hallway. She appeared back at the door a few seconds later. "Nothing. All the other rooms are empty," she said, then led Emma from the scene of destruction to the sofa. Emma sunk into the cushions, her eyes bleary.

"What we're dealing with here is a missing person," the woman said.

The male officer spoke quietly into his radio.

"Mrs Harris," — the female officer crouched in front of Emma — "we will find your husband. I'm going to ask you a few questions now."

21

Leo strained his eyes open then immediately closed them again. For once the Caribbean sunlight was unwelcome. Leo didn't think he could have been in bed for longer than five minutes. He glanced at the clock on the bedside table. It was seven thirty. Leo groaned and covered his head with the pillow. He knew he wouldn't get back to sleep now.

The night had been brilliant. They'd drank, danced and met some cool people. Now the taste of rum punch and aniseed shots engulfed his mouth.

Leo lay still and wished away the pain. His brain throbbed against the front of his skull. As expected, the throbbing didn't dissipate. Leo gave up and padded gently through to the bathroom. He swallowed two tablets, downed a glass of water and looked at himself in the mirror. Shadows bracketed his eyes, and his skin had the pallor of old pastry.

He slouched back across the room and looked out at the resort. His room was on the second floor. To the right, the pool lay empty and still. To the left, palm trees hung motionless, and the ocean sparkled hazily in the rising heat. Two hotel workers swept the sand between the sunbeds, removing footprints from the day before. A man ran past with a child in a three-wheeled buggy. Watching the activity made Leo feel nauseous.

Leo thought of Allissa sleeping two doors down. He imagined her hair spread across the pillow and the rise and fall of the duvet as she breathed. Then, the image of her in the red bikini swam into his mind. He smiled. They were just friends, but she did look good.

"Ah shit," he muttered, as he remembered today's swimming practice. There was no way the excuse of a hangover would get him out of that.

Leo finished his glass of water, downed another, then changed into his swimming shorts. Next, he draped a towel across his shoulders and wandered down to the pool. He stopped at the resort's café for two expresso shots on the way.

He would have a beer after the swimming lesson. That was the only thing that would help him now.

Leo laid his towel on a sunbed and dipped his toes in the pool's shallow end. He pulled a deep breath, counted down from three, and slipped into the water. Even the gently lapping water in the shallow end made him uncomfortable. He gripped the side and practised kicking as Allissa had shown him yesterday.

"That's it," Allissa said as she walked to the pool.

Three children slid an inflatable crocodile into the deep end and jumped in after it. Distracted by their splashes and shrieks, Leo stood up in the waist-high water. He saw Allissa in the red bikini and smiled.

Allissa removed the towel from the sunbed next to Leo's and threw it on the floor. The thought of colonisation —

even when it related to sunbeds — made her stomach roil. Though, maybe that was the hangover.

Leo thought about the person who'd placed it there, seeing Allissa now sprawled out in their spot, and giggled.

"You're doing well," Allissa said. "How're you feeling?"

"Absolutely brilliant." Leo pulled a face. The buoyant effect of the coffee was already wearing off.

"We'll have another beer in an hour," Allissa said. "That'll sort us out. After we've done some swimming."

"Sounds like a plan," Leo agreed.

Allissa jumped in the deep end with her legs tucked up beneath her. The splash reverberated across the pool.

"Right, let's do some proper strokes," Allissa said, surfacing and sweeping the hair from her face. Her skin glistened beneath the water. "Remember what you're doing there," she said, swimming towards Leo. "If you ever get stuck, just do that, and you won't drown. No need to panic ever again!"

One child, now bored with the inflatable crocodile, copied Allissa's jump. Waves pounded across the pool's surface.

"This is what we're working towards." Allissa demonstrated a slow breaststroke across the deep end. "This is a proper stroke. We're not even doing any doggy paddle. That won't get you anywhere."

Leo's phone rang from the sun lounger. He glanced towards it.

"Are you going to get that?" Allissa said.

"I suppose I should."

Leo hauled himself from the water and crossed to the sun lounger. 'Emma', Leo's sister, flashed across the phone's screen.

"Hi, Emma, you okay?" Leo said.

22

"We're going to sort this. We're going to find him," Leo said ten minutes later. They were back in Leo's room. Allissa had pulled on a strap top and shorts and sat on the bed with her laptop open.

"Start from the beginning," Leo said, taking a seat next to Allissa on the bed. "You're on speakerphone. Allissa's here too."

The conversation felt strangely familiar. It hadn't yet registered that Emma wasn't a regular client.

Emma explained the events of the previous night, culminating in her leaving to stay in the hotel.

"You're at Andy's brother's in New York?" Leo clarified. He felt terrible that he didn't even know his sister and her husband were going on holiday. He'd probably been told, but had forgotten.

"Yes, I'm here now. The police have just left."

"Is Frankie okay?"

"Yes, he's having a nap at the moment. I don't think he's even realised what's happened yet."

"You said that you guys argued last night. Is that unusual?" Leo suspected it was more common than Emma would like to admit. Leo had heard them arguing a few weeks before. Andy drank too much and got argumentative. It was a lethal combination.

Leo winced as he prepared to ask the next question. He had to. Leo needed to know what they were dealing with.

"Has Andy ever been violent towards you?"

The line went silent for a long moment.

"No," Emma finally said. "I've thought he was going to a couple of times. I've even braced myself for it. But he's never actually done it."

Allissa made a note of that.

"What sort of state was he in when you left last night?" Leo asked.

"He was angry. It was a stupid argument, really. I shouldn't have wound him up. It's my fault, really. I know what he gets like."

"No, it's not your fault," Allissa interjected. "This is all on him. None of this is your fault."

"When did you realise he'd gone?" Leo asked.

"When the police arrived earlier. I came back ready to put it behind us. I didn't want a stupid argument to ruin our holiday."

"How long are you supposed to be there?"

"Two weeks. We're spending Christmas here. Andy's brother is with his wife's family in Florida."

"And you say the car's been found?" Leo asked.

"It was a wreck in the Lincoln Tunnel. The police said they're surprised anyone could've... " Emma faltered and began sobbing.

Allissa searched for the Lincoln Tunnel on her laptop.

"It's the tunnel that connects New Jersey to Manhattan," Allissa whispered.

"Any idea where he could have been going?" Leo asked.

"No. I don't know," Emma said quietly.

Leo and Allissa's eyes met. Both knew their holiday was over. They were going to New York.

23

He couldn't believe how easy it had been. Anyone could do it. He'd planned nothing other than the locations, and he'd only chosen those for sentimental reasons. He'd just gone out, lain in wait for someone to walk past, and then...

He twisted the ancient tap, and water gushed into the basin. The decrepit plumbing protested with a series of deep metallic clangs.

He glanced around the small room. Morning light seeped through the drawn curtains. He wanted to keep the light and the prying eyes of any passers-by away. The place was simple, but it was everything he needed. No one came here anyway. Well, he smiled, no one would come here and survive.

This was the place he came to work. It was perfect. In the heart of the city, it allowed him to duck out of sight quickly.

He hadn't planned to spend the night here. But staying last night had just felt right. He didn't want to go back to his old life just yet.

It was the name that had first appealed to him — 13 Miller's Court. When he'd seen that name, he just had to acquire the place. His apartment wasn't right for this at all. Besides, it was useful to keep some separation. This was the place he came to perform the acts that ignited his passions.

He shut off the tap and stared down at the water. His reflection gazed back at him wearily. He was going to have to be careful. That, he knew. He couldn't risk not getting to his endgame. There was only one chance to do this, just one chance to avenge the memory of his great-grandfather.

He gazed up at a black and white framed picture on the wall. It was the only picture in the entire apartment. His great-grandfather, William, examined him from behind the glass, his posture rigid, and his expression fierce. Although the great man had died sixty years before his own birth — technically his great, great, great-grandfather — he felt as if they were somehow close.

He dropped the knife beneath the water. He really should have cleaned it while the blood was still wet, but he had been far too elated last night to even think about it.

The thing was, no one had any idea whether his great grandfather had been responsible for the killings. He had just been in the right place at the wrong time. He had been an eccentric man who didn't fit the mould. The sort of person those in power were happy to make an example of.

He slid his hands beneath the surface and scraped blood from the blade.

Although his great-grandfather had escaped punishment for the crimes, the fate he had served was worse. He had lost everything and died in poverty. He'd paid the ultimate price.

The knife glistened as he drew it from the basin. A vein of blood remained encrusted between the blade and the handle. He grabbed a toothbrush from the cup on the sink and used the bristles to remove it.

He knew that his great-grandfather would have hated to end his days living quietly in suburbia. That wasn't what he'd wanted at all.

"It's all for you," he said, looking up at the picture. He examined the knife. Now it sparkled flawlessly.

He smiled. That was perfect. Ready for number three.

24

Leo juddered with anxiety as the plane's nose dipped and they descended towards New York.

Lost in the hazy half-sleep he could only ever manage on flights, the change in direction caused his mind to jump into a panic. His eyes shot open, expecting a scene of chaos as they plummeted towards the ocean below.

Of course, everything was as it should be. Normal and serene. Leo took a deep breath and stretched as best he could in the confines of the seat. Allissa slept beside him. She snored lightly with her head tilted to the side. Leo let the breath go, and his anxiety faded.

Everything was fine.

Leo had suffered from anxiety for years. It came sporadically, with no logic or reason. Sometimes weeks would pass without an attack. Other times, two in the same day would tear through his consciousness.

He gazed out the window and thought about the investigation that would start as soon as they landed in the Big Apple.

Over the years, Leo had tried many things to deal with

his anxiety; drugs, therapy, and some strange alternative remedies he'd found online. Although the anxiety still plagued him, now he knew how to deal with it. First, he knew that, however bad the anxiety was, he would survive. Second, he found Allissa's company calming. She stopped the world from closing in around him.

"Are we nearly there?" Allissa mumbled, stirring from her sleep. She pulled out her earphones and glanced at Leo.

"Yeah, coming into land soon," Leo said, peering at the battalion of grey buildings below.

The action film Leo had attempted to watch before dozing reached its climax on the small screen. The band of superheroes appeared to be winning against the black-clad villains. It was a simple fight, good versus evil, and all set in a world where you could tell a character's intentions by their clothes.

It would be so much easier if things were like that, Leo thought. If you could just tell who the villains and heroes were by the way they appeared.

Yet, then again, maybe you could.

Leo had never liked Andy. Even when Emma had first introduced him to Leo years earlier, Leo hadn't liked him. Leo didn't think the man was dangerous to begin with. Leo just thought he was a bit of a dick. The thought of him being aggressive, perhaps violent, had only occurred to Leo during a recent visit to Andy and Emma's house. Maybe if Leo had done something about it then, perhaps this would never have happened.

On the screen a car flipped over, and a group of people ran for cover. Leo wondered what happened to the evil characters after the heroes won. Did they get some kind of rehabilitation? Did they get a second chance at being good, or was that it? Changing the villains into advocates for good would be the real victory.

Leo wondered if that would happen when they found Andy. Would he get another chance? Leo hoped so. He wanted to make Andy see that he was turning his back on a woman and a young boy who loved him.

Leo was confident they could find a man like Andy. He was less optimistic that Andy would ever be the man Leo's sister and nephew deserved.

25

Across the wide radiance of the Hudson River, the towers of Manhattan stretched into the cerulean afternoon sky. The urgency of the city faded on this side of the river. It was as though the city's chaos couldn't make it through the tunnel.

"This is it?" Leo asked the taxi driver as they stopped outside a large and modern apartment building on Wellington Avenue.

"That's the one." The driver pointed at the building's grand entrance.

Leo paid the taxi with his credit card, wincing at the price. They wouldn't usually take a taxi that distance, but time was short today.

Allissa thanked the driver, got out, and stared up at the building. "Cool place," she said.

Andy's brother was waiting for them as the lift doors opened.

"We came back as soon as we heard," Michael said. "Left the kids at the parents' in Orlando. We just want to be here for Em."

New York

Leo had only met Michael once, at Emma and Andy's wedding.

Michael was clearly Andy's brother. They looked alike, except Michael kept his sandy hair in a messy style and wore thick-framed glasses.

"Good to see you again," Michael said, shaking Leo's hand. "Shame it's in these circumstances."

Leo introduced Allissa, then Michael led them into the apartment.

"Thank you for coming so quickly," Michael said. "The police are looking too, but I know you guys are experts at this. I've been following your cases. Impressive stuff."

Leo and Allissa followed Michael through a brightly-lit hallway and into the apartment's open-plan living space. Allissa took in the view and nodded. It was a very cool apartment. She turned away from the window and sat on the large leather sofa. The place was slightly reminiscent of an apartment from which they'd rescued a young woman in Hong Kong. This one was more colourful though, with patterned cushions and a print of Warhol's Marilyn Monroe on the wall.

Emma was sitting with a slim, black-haired woman. Emma glanced at Leo and smiled weakly. Her skin was pale, and shadows bracketed her eyes.

"We came as quickly as we could," Leo said, hugging Emma as she stood up.

"Thank you, thank you." Emma pushed her face into Leo's shoulder.

Leo put his arms around her. She felt frail and vulnerable. Anger at the man who'd caused this pain welled up inside Leo.

Emma took a deep breath and pulled away. "Thank you for coming, I just didn't know what else to do."

"This is my wife, Nadia," Michael said.

Nadia smiled from Leo to Allissa, then folded her arms.

"Is there anything we can do to help you?" Michael asked.

"We just need to know as much as possible," Allissa told him. "That'll give us the best chance of finding Andy."

Leo sat next to Emma. She examined her hands.

Allissa verbally ran through what they already knew.

"That's it exactly," Emma said. "I just got back in the morning, and he wasn't here. I didn't notice anything until the police turned up."

"What did he take with him?" Allissa asked.

Nadia straightened up uncomfortably.

"Nothing, really. His suitcase is here. He took some of Michael's clothes, that's it."

"Is his passport here?" Leo asked.

Emma nodded.

Nadia squirmed.

"Wallet? Credit cards? Money?" Allissa said.

"Nope, all here."

"He can't have gone that far then," Leo said. "He wouldn't be able to afford —"

"You've got to tell them," Nadia declared, staring at Michael. She spoke in the broad tones of a native New Yorker.

Michael glanced at her. If the interjection annoyed him, he didn't show it.

"Tell us what?" Allissa asked.

"Okay," Michael said, putting a hand on his wife's forearm. "I didn't tell the police this because I didn't want Andy to be in any more trouble, and honestly, it doesn't really matter. He took some of the cash we keep in the apartment for emergencies."

"How much —"

"Two thousand dollars," Nadia cut in.

Leo's eyebrows raised.

"Yeah, it's not a problem at all. We'd have given it to him if he'd asked wouldn't we Nadia?" Michael looked at his wife. She didn't seem sure.

"Okay, thanks for telling us that," Allissa said. "That changes the sort of places we'll look."

"He took your car as well?" Leo asked.

"Yes. We assume so, at least. Police found the car around two in the morning in the Lincoln Tunnel. Totally smashed up. Unrecognisable. Much to their surprise, it was empty. How anyone could've walked away from a wreck like that, they didn't know. Sorry," Michael added, glancing at Emma.

Allissa nodded and made a note on her phone.

"We're not worried about the car, or the money," Michael confirmed. "We just want to know that Andy's okay."

Nadia crossed her arms and turned away from her husband. *She seems more concerned than Michael*, Leo thought.

Emma whimpered from the sofa beside Leo.

"Is there anything we can do to help?" Michael asked again as Leo and Allissa stood to leave.

Leo looked at Emma. He wanted to stay and be with her, but Andy wouldn't get found that way.

"We'll look after her, don't worry," Nadia said, seeing Leo's turmoil. "You go and look for that guy. We all want a word with him."

"Do you need somewhere to stay or something?" Michael asked.

"We booked a place yesterday, but thanks."

"Have you got —"

"Yes, we've got everything we need to get started," Allissa confirmed, heading for the door.

"Okay," Michael said. "Oh, if you need a bit of local help, a friend of ours used someone, didn't they?" Andy glanced at Nadia. "What were they called?"

"Niki Zadid," she said.

"Yes, that was it. I can look up the contact details for you now if you —"

"Got it," Allissa said, typing into her phone. "That could be useful. Having a person who knows the area is always helpful."

"I can imagine. And I'm paying the bill. No arguments on that."

"Sure." Leo hugged Emma and shook Michael's hand. "We'll be in touch soon. If you think of anything else that might be useful, let us know."

26

Local knowledge counted for everything when trying to track someone down. Cases were lost or won on what you knew about the location and its people.

"I'm not saying we shouldn't get help," Leo said as the metro rumbled beneath Manhattan. "I just think we should think about what we can do on our own first."

"No," Allissa said. "We can't afford to waste time. We need to get this detective on the case as soon as possible. He'll know where to look. He'll have all the contacts. Remember when you were looking for me in Kathmandu? What was the first thing you did?"

"Okay," Leo conceded. Allissa was right. The first thing he'd done on arriving in Kathmandu was contact someone who knew the city, the local customs, and could speak the language. Tau had been invaluable. Leo likely wouldn't have found Allissa or survived the ordeal without him.

"What do we know about this detective then?" Leo asked as Allissa thumbed the bell of Niki Zadid's office in Greenwich Village. The office was on the third floor of a townhouse in a wide, quiet, and tree-lined street. The area felt a long way from the famous spires of the Empire State and Chrysler buildings, which pierced the skyline to the north, and the World Trade Centre, which cast its long shadow from the south.

"Not a lot, really. But Michael recommended him. His website lists all sorts of things, marital stuff, missing people, research for legal cases, that sort of thing."

An electronic taxi hissed beneath the skeletal trees behind them. Allissa stepped back and stared up at the four-storey building. To their left, people sat at the outside tables of a café, despite the cold.

"Maybe he's not in," Leo said. "Might be out on a case or something. We should have got an appointment."

"Yeah. We were passing anyway, though. Let's try again."

Leo pressed the buzzer a second time. He put his ear close to the door but couldn't hear the bell. Music played from somewhere inside the building. Leo leant against the door and put his ear to the glass. One song faded and the next began. The bass rattled through the building. He couldn't hear anything else.

The door clicked and swung open. Leo tried to stand up but wasn't quick enough. He fell into the arms of a lady with long blonde hair.

"Watch where you're going will ya!" she said, not expecting to get an arm full of unkempt and confused English detective as she stepped outside.

"Sorry, sorry!" Leo said, pulling himself away and blushing.

Allissa tried and failed to stifle a laugh.

"Quick, the door," Allissa said as the woman marched away.

Leo put his foot inside the frame to stop the door swinging closed.

"Let's have a look," Allissa said, pushing past him.

"I suppose." Leo followed Allissa into the grand hallway. "A locked door has never stopped us before."

Leo followed Allissa up the stairs, and thought of their flat's stuffy entrance hall. In Brighton they had piles of junk mail and rusting bikes. Here they had a sleek tiled floor and ornate furniture.

The music got louder as they climbed the stairs. The deep thud of a kick drum and a bouncing bassline reminded Leo of the club he'd visited a few weeks ago in Berlin. On the third floor, the walls shook from thumping bass. A black and white framed photograph of a group of men unloading a train bounced against its fixings.

Allissa paused and turned to face Leo. A brass plaque beside the door indicated the office of *N. Zadid P.I.*

The music was coming from inside.

Leo was disappointed that the name wasn't in silver letters on a glass door, like in a famous detective novel, though he still expected to find Niki with his feet on the desk, smoking a cigar and drinking whiskey.

Allissa knocked on the door. Grunting bass swamped the sound. No response. Allissa tried again, this time rapping on the door as hard as she could. Nothing happened for a moment, and then the music stopped.

Leo and Allissa glanced at each other. The door didn't move. Allissa knocked again.

"Come in!"

Allissa pushed open the door and stepped into the room.

"Wow," Allissa whispered, looking around.

Prints of modern art covered the pastel blue walls. A

chandelier hung from the high ceiling. Sumptuous sofas gathered around a glass coffee table. Bookshelves covered the wall at one end of the room, and windows overlooked the street at the other. The maps, documents and photographs spread across the coffee table indicated the occupant's profession.

"Can I help you?" came a woman's voice in a bold New York accent. She slid an enormous book from the bottom shelf and stood. Without looking at the intruders, she leafed through the book until she found the page she wanted, then tapped it thoughtfully. She was slight, short, moved with bird-like efficiency and wore a bright blue hijab which covered her hair and flowed down her back. Her clothes, although modest, had a fashionable cut. She gave the impression that nothing about her appearance was an accident.

"Yes, I hope so," Leo said. "We're looking for Niki Zadid."

"Why?" the woman asked. She crossed the room and laid the book on top of one of the maps on the coffee table.

"We're missing people investigators," Allissa told her. "We've got to find someone in New York. We're looking for —"

"Is Niki about?" Leo said.

The woman flicked forward two pages and then glanced up at Leo.

"Is this guy shitting me?" she barked, looking at Allissa. "You wanna talk to Niki, huh?" She stood upright. "Who do you think you're looking at?"

Allissa laughed out loud, and Niki's expression broke into a lopsided grin. Leo blushed.

"I'm so sorry —"

"Leave it, Sherlock," Niki cut in. "A lesson for the future. You go into someone's office, and their fucking name's on the door, who's the person you're most likely to find there? It's not a trick question." Niki grinned, and the left side of her mouth moved higher than the right.

Leo blushed.

"Don't worry," Niki said when Leo tried to apologise again. "To be honest, that's why I'm good at my job. No one expects this." She tugged on the hijab. "Coffee?"

"You have a beautiful office," Allissa said accepting a cup of coffee from Niki.

"Thanks. Yeah, I do alright. There are a lot of rich people in this city, and rich people don't trust each other. It seems they spend half their time trying to make money and the other half worrying about losing it. So, they hire me."

"Sounds good," Leo said. "Seriously though, sorry —"

"Drop it," Niki declared, raising her hand. "As I said, it helps with the job. You pair don't look much like detectives, either." Niki glanced from Leo to Allissa and back again.

"No, I suppose not," Leo agreed.

"What do you need then?" Niki leaned back into the sofa. Her personality seemed to take up more space than her slim figure occupied. Allissa calculated her age as somewhere in her early forties.

Leo and Alissa explained the situation.

"You got a name?"

"Yeah, Andy Harris," Allissa said. She unlocked and scrolled through her phone. "Here's a photo."

"Okay." Niki dug a wafer-thin laptop from beneath a map on the table and opened it. The laptop was about a third the size of Allissa's. "Send me that picture," Niki said, her fingers flashing over the keys.

Leo examined the map on the table. It was a section of Manhattan, which Niki had marked with two crosses. A pile of books on famous serial killers lay open to one side.

"Describe this Andy character to me," Niki said without looking up.

Leo gave Niki all the background information he thought was relevant. Niki's phone beeped. She grabbed it from the tabletop.

"Sorry," Niki said, "I've just gotta check this." She tapped a few keys, and a picture appeared on a large screen on the wall. A young man with a wave of brown hair and intense grey eyes was speaking to a TV news reporter.

"Bastard," Niki muttered. "How does he know so much?"

"What's that?" Allissa asked.

"Two girls were murdered last night, and it looks like the work of a serial killer. They've already named him the Downtown Ripper." Niki pointed at the screen. "This guy writes for a true crime blog. If they're interviewing him about it, then the police haven't told them anything. They're just going to have to wait and see what happens."

"Are you looking into it?" Allissa asked.

"Hell yeah," Niki said as she looked at Allissa, "and if I get there before the NYPD on a case like this, then I won't have to do the bidding of suspicious housewives ever again."

The man on the screen spoke for a couple of minutes about the murders.

"Alright," Niki said, snapping off the screen and flashing Leo and Allissa her lopsided smile. "I'll look into it for you. I'll call you tomorrow. And be careful out there. New York city can be a dangerous place."

27

When you're about to die, your life flashes before your eyes — that's what Andy had heard, anyway. Those final moments give you time to question the decisions you've made and the chances you've taken. They give you the opportunity, in total freedom, to find peace with your worldly shortcomings and discover something positive, happy and fulfilling.

This would have happened to Andy if he wasn't so drunk. He'd been drinking all day. There were the beers at the airport, then on the plane, then the crate he'd bought at the shop. Finally, the bottle of whiskey. Considering that, as the Porsche spun through the tunnel at eighty miles per hour, all Andy could think about were the events of the last few hours. But it didn't really matter. He wouldn't remember it anyway.

Andy opened his eyes slowly. Light tore into his retinas.

"Turn off the lights, will you?" he muttered. His voice was croaky and weak. It didn't sound like him at all.

The lights continued to blaze. Andy swore and strained his eyes closed again. Colours danced across his eyelids. His head throbbed.

Usually, vague memories joined the dancing colours by now. Andy lay still and tried to think. No memories came forth. His mind remained blank. That was unusual.

He rubbed his face with the palms of his hands. His skin felt rough and dusty.

A glass of water, a strong coffee and some headache pills — that's what he needed now.

"Emma, get me —" Andy shouted. That would sort him right out. Then he'd be able to open his eyes and work out what day it was.

He didn't have work, did he? Andy felt a sudden confusion. No, he was sure he didn't have to go to work. He wouldn't have got in this state on a work night.

"Emma!" Andy shouted again.

Then Andy heard a voice reply. It wasn't Emma's.

"Who you callin' Emma?" replied the voice. It was deep — a man. It had an accent. American.

Andy pushed himself upright and opened his eyes. The light seared a hole straight into his brain. Andy jammed his eyes closed and rested back on his elbows. Every inch of his body ached. There was something seriously wrong with this bed. He just couldn't get comfortable.

"I'm talkin' to you, boy," the man said again. "Who you callin' Emma?"

Andy drew a deep breath. He'd heard of people hearing voices, but he'd never known that on a hangover. He really should stop drinking so much.

"First you take my place, now you're ignoring me, boy. Well, that ain't happening."

A pair of thick hands pulled Andy to his feet. His brain protested at the movement. Every muscle ached.

"Hey, what, you can't... wait..." Andy struggled to form words. The additional movement caused too much pain. He opened his eyes and tried to look around. The light stung and his brain thumped.

"Na, you've been here all night, boy, snoring like a train and shouting for Emma. None of us got a wink of sleep."

Andy turned towards the voice's owner. His eyes finally focused. A tall and wiry black man held him by the arm. Andy struggled to keep upright. The man dragged Andy forwards. He felt a fresh wave of pain.

"Where am I? What... who..."

He glanced around. The focus of his vision improved. They were walking through some kind of tunnel or underground car park. Occasional bulbs lit cold concrete walls and sleeping figures covered the floor.

"Oh, it's like that now, is it?" the man said. "You show up here and make use of our fine hospitality, and then you don't remember a thing."

"I'm... I am..." Andy stuttered, but the words felt alien. His tongue was too big for his mouth.

The man pulled Andy around a person sleeping on the floor. His bed was a piece of cardboard laid flat on the concrete.

"Where am I?" Andy asked.

"You'll see," the man told him.

The tunnel turned slightly, became lighter, then inclined steeply. Andy gazed towards the light and tried to make out what was up there. The light was too bright. He saw nothing.

"Go that way," the man said, pointing up the ramp. "First

you owe me for the liquor last night." He held out a sizeable, gnarled hand.

"What liquor?"

"Of course," the man said, "you had at least your fair share. Ten dollars." His hand closed and opened again.

"Dollars?" Andy asked. "Where am I?"

The man smiled, showing two brown teeth.

"This isn't Kansas anymore, Dorothy." He tilted his head back and cackled towards the ceiling. "Ten dollars, now."

Andy tapped his pockets.

"Or I'll be taking that nice jacket of yours." The man tugged on Andy's lapel.

Andy looked at it. He didn't recognise the jacket.

Andy pulled a note from his pocket and unfolded it. It was a dollar bill. He passed it to the man.

"No way, more than that," the man said. "What am I gonna buy with that? A fucking lollypop?"

Andy searched his pockets and pulled out a roll of notes. He unfurled them. They were one-hundred-dollar bills, a stack of them. Andy separated one from the bunch and gave it to the man.

The man showed his near-toothless gums and accepted the hundred dollar bill.

"It's a pleasure doin' business with ya," he said, folding the money out of sight. "If you just follow the road up that way, you'll see where you are. Come back anytime you like."

Andy turned on shaking legs and stumbled up the ramp. His body ached with each step. The further he went, the brighter the light became.

Andy reached the mouth of the tunnel and stared out. The world around him shook. He took a hard intake of breath as recognition dawned. He put his hand above his eyes to shield himself from the sun and stared upwards. The surrounding buildings ran towards the sky.

Then the spell broke. The noise of the city blared. A yellow taxi shot past and music thumped from somewhere down the road. Andy knew what city this was. But how he got here, he did not understand.

28

"We should be out there looking." Leo stopped and turned to face Allissa. "We need to get on this straight away. Check hospitals, hotels, squats – anywhere someone could disappear in the city. We don't have time to lose on this case."

Allissa stared at the colourful street around them and down to the map on her phone. They were now in Chinatown, having walked across Manhattan from Niki's office in Greenwich Village. Allissa always thought the best way to get to know a new place was on foot. Maps and pictures offered nothing, compared to seeing the landscape of a place unfold at street level.

"What, just go around New York randomly asking people?" she said, tucking her phone away. "That could take us weeks. We don't even know where to start yet."

"But we have to start." Leo pictured Emma, weak and vulnerable, crumpled into the sofa.

A neon sign snapped on and bathed the street in pink.

"We've just got to do something, haven't we?" Leo stepped in front of Allissa and then turned to face her.

"Yes. We'll get some food, have a beer, talk about what we know, then get a decent night's sleep. I don't know about you, but I'm starving. It feels like last night we were at that street party."

They passed a restaurant and the hiss of frying noodles tumbled into the street. Allissa paused. The only other customers were a group of Chinese teenagers drinking brightly-coloured drinks at the back table.

"Come on," Allissa said, pulling Leo inside. "Let's eat, everything feels better with food."

Leo slumped down at the table by the window. Two cars rumbled past the mist-mottled glass. Night had fallen now, but neon signs, hanging haphazardly from the buildings, washed the street in vibrant and chaotic colours.

Allissa returned with two bottles of Tsingtao.

"I've just ordered us a range of stuff," she said. "All sorts. You'll like it."

"Thanks," Leo said, picking up the bottle.

"We'll make some progress tomorrow," Allissa said. "Don't worry. We've found people all over the world now. We can do this."

"I know, I know," Leo said, taking a sip. "But this time it's Emma, you know?"

Allissa nodded. "This time it's personal. That's why we need rest first."

Leo nodded absently. On a large TV, a newscaster faded and the image of an alleyway between two shops appeared. Police tape fluttered in the breeze and two men wheeled a stretcher towards an ambulance.

Leo took another sip. He knew they'd found people in more chaotic and mysterious circumstances than this, but for some reason, New York gave him a bad feeling.

29

He was in New York. It just didn't make any sense. Andy was in New York.

Stumbling down the pavement — what was it they called them here? Sidewalks? — he tried to take it all in. Crowds of people hustled around him, traffic thronged, and noise blared. It was cold but bright. Andy shivered and pulled the jacket tightly around him. He glanced down at the jacket but didn't recognise that either.

"Hey, watch out!" a man shouted, pushing past Andy.

Andy didn't recognise any of his clothes. They didn't look like his. They were dirty, too. He'd have to get cleaned up.

Andy didn't live here. He knew where he lived — a village near Bristol. In England! So, what the hell was he doing here?

There's some strange shit going on, he thought.

Andy scanned the surrounding street. His eyes alighted on the glimmering lights of a bar across the road. His protesting legs told him he needed to sit down and work out what was going on. He hustled across the road, pushed open the door of Madison's Corner Café, and stepped inside. Hits of the nineties thumped from the soundsystem, and half a dozen giant TV screens showed various sporting fixtures. Along the bar, a few people sat eating and drinking by the glow of the beer taps. The place was gloomy and cavernous, and smelled of beer. Exactly what Andy needed.

Andy shook the chill from his fingers and walked up to the bar.

"What can I get ya?" the barman asked.

Andy pushed the circling doubts from his mind. Everything felt better in here.

"The Brooklyn Lager, please," Andy said. "And a whiskey chaser."

"Coming up," the guy said, selecting a bottle, then filling a glass and sliding it onto the bar.

Andy lifted the glass and swallowed it straight down.

"Nicely done," the man sat beside him at the bar said. "Been one of those days?"

Andy hopped up onto the barstool and looked at the man. He was big, older than Andy and dressed unmistakably like a cowboy. A wide-brimmed Stetson drooped low over his eyes.

"Hell yeah," Andy said, dropping the glass to the bar. "Another in there, please."

"I'll have one too," said the man beside him. "And it's my round. The name's Otto," the cowboy said, offering his hand. Andy accepted it. The next round of whiskeys arrived.

"Shall I put it on your tab, Otto?" the barman asked.

"Sure thing Zach, you do that," Otto replied. "What brings you to New York?" he asked Andy.

Andy took his first sip of the Brooklyn Lager. He was feeling better already. Andy was used to waking up with sections of his memory missing — what difference did this make?

"Just a few days away," Andy said.

"Good place for it." Otto raised a tall glass containing orange liquid and clinked it with Andy's. "Been to New York before?"

"No." Andy didn't think he had. Nothing seemed that familiar.

"It's a great place. You'll like it." Otto finished his drink and pushed the empty glass across the bar. "Zach, sort us another round."

"The usual?"

"Sure, plus whatever this guy's having."

Andy gazed up at the six large screens showing various sports and news.

"Ah man, not this again," Otto said, pointing towards one screen.

"What's that?" Andy asked.

"Some idiot's gone and killed two women on their way home last night. Just for no reason. Pretty gruesome, too. They're calling him The Downtown Ripper."

Images of fluttering crime scene tape and police cars flashed across the screen.

"This sort of thing happen often?"

"People get killed all the time, sure, but this has the makings of a serial killer. Apparently, the victims aren't connected. Different parts of the city. Bodies left in different places."

The barman put two more whiskeys in front of Andy and the cowboy.

"He cut them up a bit too," Otto said, lifting the whiskey to his lips.

Andy looked at the man.

"Yeah." Otto ran his index finger from his stomach up to his neck. "Proper took them apart, know what I'm saying?"

"That's gross." Andy downed the whiskey in one.

"Oh, and this guy..." Otto pointed with the same index finger towards the screen. "They always get him on when there's some kind of murder. Thinks he knows it all."

"Who is he?"

"Some true crime blogger or some shit. He's not even published in a proper newspaper or anything. But, I s'pose that doesn't matter anymore. He's pretty famous for it, apparently."

Andy watched the man on the screen. He must have been in his early twenties, with a styled wave of thick brown hair and cold grey eyes.

"Anyway, we don't need to worry about that," Otto said, lifting the whiskey.

"Why's that?" Andy asked.

"It seems he only likes girls. Cheers!"

30

Tonight, things were going to go down a little differently. He was going to enjoy tonight even more. He looked at himself in the mirror and smiled. He knew that he had a certain look about him. A look that got him a lot of attention. The right kind of attention. And tonight, he was going to use that to his advantage.

Although the plan last night had worked — he had, after all, found two women and done what he'd wanted — he hadn't been able to *choose* them. He'd got lucky with the first one. She was beautiful. *Was!*

He closed his eyes and pictured her naked porcelain figure. The image hadn't left his mind all day. He ran his fingers across the bracelet on his left wrist and bit his lower lip. He wanted them all to look like that. He *needed* them to look like that.

The problem was, if he simply lay in wait for someone to pass, then he just had to take whoever turned up. There was too much luck involved. He didn't know who was going to pass, nor whether they would be to his specific tastes.

This way, he thought, pulling on his blazer, he got to

New York

choose exactly who he wanted. He also knew, as they had many times before, that they would follow him wherever he wanted to go.

Of course, there was always a risk that someone would see them leaving or that there would be CCTV, something like that. Yet he knew for a fact that the Opus Jazz Club didn't have CCTV inside — that was its appeal for the sort of people who frequented it. It was just around the corner from his next location.

It was unusual for a serial killer to change their M.O. like this. But, that was the beauty of it. He could slip through the doors of the city's most elite nightclubs, and no one would think twice. That was better than hiding in an alleyway and waiting for a victim. This way, he could choose carefully. He could select someone he wanted to spend time with.

He examined his apartment. It was so different from the grimy room he used to clean up after his crimes. This place was clean, simple, and most importantly, normal. There was nothing to indicate his intentions or desires. That was the way he should be. It annoyed him that people with the compulsion to kill were always portrayed in such animalistic terms. There wasn't anything animalistic about it. It was a passion — like any other. A passion that burned inside him. A passion that he suspected had run through his family for generations.

He brought the gold bracelet to his mouth and kissed it.

"I'll make you proud," he whispered.

His phone buzzed. The taxi was outside.

31

"How long you in New York for?" Otto said as Andy followed him from the bar and into the back of a waiting taxi.

"Crazy thing," Andy said. "I don't know."

"Opus Jazz Club," Otto said to the driver before folding himself into the taxi's back seat.

Night had fallen now. Andy realised they must have been in the bar for hours. The lightness of booze had replaced the throbbing pain in his body. He felt good.

"How can you not know?" Otto asked as the taxi slid from the kerb. Andy watched the vibrant activity of night-time New York and grinned. He was in one of the most exciting cities in the world, and was now off to some exclusive club. Whatever his life had been like before, it wasn't as good as this.

Andy explained the events of the morning.

"That's crazy man," Otto said. "You can't remember anything?"

"Not yet, though I reckon it'll all come back. For now, I'm just going to enjoy it. I'm not sure why, but I get the feeling that the reason I'm here was sort of stressful. You know what I mean?"

"Yeah, I getcha." Otto nodded.

The taxi turned a corner and slowed to a crawl. The buildings in this part of the city were older. Their shadows hung low across the streets. Steam billowed from a grate in the middle of the street.

"Thanks, keep it," Otto said as he gave the driver a folded note and got out of the taxi. He glanced at the sky and shivered. "S'posed to snow in the next couple days."

"Where're we going?" Andy asked, standing from the taxi. He suddenly felt unsteady and held on to the car's roof for support. They had drunk a lot already.

"I come here almost every night," Otto said. "It's one of the best venues in the city."

Otto crossed the road and headed towards an unassuming door. Two burly doormen stood either side of the entrance. At least a dozen people queued behind a rope.

"Hey Otto!" one doorman said, shaking Otto's hand. "You brought a guest tonight?" The doorman folded his arms across his broad chest.

"Sure," Otto said. "Andy. He's just in the city for a few days. Figured I'd show him around."

The doorman pulled the rope aside. Andy followed Otto into the club.

32

He used to love the welcome of the rope being moved aside. He used to think it was one of the best feelings in the city. That was, until last night. Everything paled into insignificance compared to last night.

He paused and looked back at the people in the queue. One woman caught his eye. Her long blonde hair cascaded over a sparkling silver dress. His eyes slunk across her body. Yes, she would do. She would do nicely. He smiled and brushed his right thigh where his trousers concealed the knife.

He thanked the doorman by name and stepped inside. People knew who he was and wouldn't even think about searching him. That just wasn't the done thing. He used to be one of the people waiting in the queue outside. Not anymore. Not since people had started listening to him.

He entered the room to a kaleidoscope of sound. Latin piano drifted above bongos and a bass guitar. The band were well into their set. The clunk and tinkle of cocktail

New York

production echoed from the bar, and hushed voices drifted from the booths at the back.

Many of the booths were already full, the faces of their occupants almost invisible in the low lights. Bottles and glasses shimmered. A wisp of smoke curled upwards from a freshly made cocktail.

"Would you like a table today, sir?" the host asked.

He had already walked into the crowd.

It was time to hunt.

33

"Your bottle, sir." The host slid a bottle of tequila onto the table, with two glasses and a bucket of ice. "Would you like anything to mix it with?"

"No, thank you," Otto said, picking up the bottle and pulling out the stopper. He turned to Andy. "That's how they do things here, you buy the bottle, and then they'll keep it for you. I only started this one yesterday." Otto held the bottle up to the light. The golden liquid within it sparkled.

Andy examined the club with child-like amazement.

A pair of young women with shimmering drinks stood at the bar. The small dancefloor was already full of young and beautiful people twisting to the music.

"Cool place ain't it," Otto declared, sliding a glass of tequila across to Andy.

Although the music was loud, they could still hold a conversation in the booth.

"Yeah, I like it," Andy said, watching a pair of women pick their way across the room. A pop echoed from the bar, and a cloud of smoke drifted from a cocktail glass.

"That stuff's all for show," Otto said, "but the young

things like it. They like to take pictures of their drinks and whatever. That's the way things are now, I s'pose."

As though on cue, a woman in a silver dress removed a smartphone from her bag and snapped a picture of her drink as it billowed thick white smoke.

"We get many famous people in here too," Otto said. "Film stars, singers, all that. That's the kind of place it is. But don't be fooled by them. Some of them have got nothing to spend at all. The people you've never heard of, they're the ones with the most money."

Andy lifted the glass to his lips.

"You see that guy?" Otto pointed towards a guy in the booth next to theirs. "He's the prince of some Middle Eastern country. He spends about three months over here, and when he does, he's in here every night. And that guy," — Otto pointed to another man — "his family owns about a third of the city. You wouldn't recognise them out on the street at all. I suppose that's the way they like it."

Andy leaned back into the seat. The drink warmed his throat. Whatever he'd forgotten, he doubted it was as good as this.

34

"Hey," he said, and smiled as the woman in a shiny silver dress pushed past him at the bar.

He'd been watching her for the last few minutes. She, he had to admit, was perfect. Her skin was the colour of marble, and her hair was long.

Her eyes widened as they met his. A twinge of recognition, possibly. He held her gaze. She wouldn't look away now.

"Hey, aren't you..." she said, her voice soft and sibilant.

"No, of course not." His mouth twisted into a smile. The game was on.

"You're not?"

"That depends." He took a deep swig from his bottle of beer and lifted himself from the stool. The knife moved beneath the fabric of his trousers. Excitement trembled through him.

"Not what?"

"Who you think I am."

"Aren't you that guy from —"

"Well, I need another drink right now." He raised his bottle to the barman. "Do you need another one too?"

"I'm supposed to be here with my friends."

"I don't think they'll mind, do you?"

She glanced over her shoulder. The group she'd left a few minutes before were dancing on the far side of the room. None of them looked in her direction.

"Sure," she said, showing a row of perfect white teeth. "I'll have another one of these."

35

Sitting in the booth and looking out at the nightclub, Andy got the feeling he used to do things like this frequently. That he used to go out and dance and drink. That he used to enjoy it. He relished the adventure of a good night out. Yet, that hadn't happened in a while, and he couldn't remember why.

"Come on," Otto said, draining his glass. "You've got to keep up. That's the rules." Otto tipped the bottle, ready to refill Andy's glass. Andy took a deep breath. The room wobbled, then spun. Andy blinked. His eyes were dry.

"No excuses," Otto said, tilting the bottle further.

Andy nodded and poured the contents of the glass down his throat.

"Good man," Otto said. His face appeared carved from granite beneath the shadowed brim of his Stetson. Otto refilled both their glasses. "Nice to meet someone who can keep up," Otto said, tapping his glass against Andy's.

36

"These things are all show," he said, passing the drink across to the woman in the shimmering dress. "Don't you think?"

"I think they taste nice too," she said, finishing the latest one. She was on her fifth or sixth now — he'd lost count. They sat in one of the shadowed booths at the back of the club. A private corner. A night just for two.

The band played frantically, but he didn't notice.

He knew her name, where she worked and what she was doing here, but those things weren't important. Getting her to leave with him — that was the important part. She leant heavily on the table. His eyes scanned her body. Yes. She was perfect.

"Yeah, but all this smoke and stuff," he said, leaning towards her. "You don't need that, do you?"

"I like it," she said, examining him through bleary eyes. She rubbed the stem of the cocktail glass between finger and thumb. Her nails glistened like the blade of his knife.

"As long as it keeps you happy," he said, finishing his drink.

"Are you sure I don't know you?" she asked, her eyes narrowing on him. "I swear I've seen you somewhere before."

"Maybe we live on the same street?"

She pouted and talked about where she lived.

She won't be going back there, he thought, listening intently.

He was purposefully vague in reply. That intrigued her further.

"Well, that can't be it then. How do you think you know me?"

"Can't remember," she said, taking another sip of the drink. She'd almost finished this one, too.

"I just think I've just got one of those faces." He shuffled closer to her in the booth. "You could get to know me if you wanted." He reached beneath the table and put his hand on her bare thigh.

She smiled and turned. Her eyes glowed, promising all that was to come.

He leaned in and kissed her. He inhaled her scent. The knife pressed against his skin. Its steel blade tantalised him. The night was going just as he'd hoped.

"We'd need to go somewhere a little quieter," he said, leaning back again. It was all part of the game.

"For what?"

"To get to know each other a little bit better."

"Do you have anywhere in mind?" Her soft words begged for more.

"I know just the place," he said, standing up. "I'll pay the bill and meet you outside in five minutes."

The frosty night air slapped his face as he stepped from the club. The band was a distant grumble now and the dozy city of the early morning murmured around him.

New York

"Good night sir," the doorman said.

He nodded at the doorman and strode away. Once out of sight, he leant against the wall of a closed café. He didn't have to wait long.

"I thought you weren't coming," he said. She pulled her coat tighter around her.

His breath rose in great clouds through the early morning air.

"Queue for the cloakroom," she said. "I'm looking forward to seeing this quiet place of yours."

"Oh, you'll like it." He placed his hand on the base of her back. "You'll like it very much."

37

Leo gazed around the room for a few moments before realising where he was. The room, all orange and green, attacked his early morning sensibilities. Light piled in from the large window and a discoloured ceiling fan spun lackadaisically.

Allissa slept soundly in her matching single bed across the room.

Leo checked the time. It was seven-thirty. He found not being able to sleep late endlessly frustrating. Wherever they were, whatever time zone or whatever place, Leo always seemed to wake up early. And once he was awake, that was that.

He got out of bed and padded across to the window. He peered between the curtains at the street below. Chinatown was already busy. The shops on the opposite side of the road spilled out onto pavements. A taxi honked as it struggled to pass two men unloading a truck.

Leo turned away from the window and examined the small room. It wasn't the luxury they'd enjoyed in the

New York

Caribbean, but they were covering the costs for this case. No wealthy sponsor was paying their expenses this time.

He padded to the bathroom, filled a glass with water and eyed himself in the mirror. He would go for a run. That would wake him up and energise him for the day. Back in Brighton, he ran almost every day. Running helped him to put things into perspective. While his legs pounded the tarmac and his lungs filled with the sea air of the English Channel, he could find solutions to problems that would otherwise have plagued him. If the case was troubling him, or he needed to work something out, the best thing he could do was pull on his trainers and head out for a run.

Leo sat on the end of the bed and rummaged through his backpack for his running clothes and shoes. He'd made sure to pack them this time. He'd imagined himself getting in a few miles along the St Lucian beaches. Not the streets of Manhattan, though.

Leo tied the laces of his trainers and thought about where someone like Andy might go in New York. That was the problem he wanted to solve first.

He stepped out on to the busy streets of Chinatown and turned right. He had no idea where to go, but right seemed as good as left. An unseen train rumbled high above him towards the Manhattan Bridge. Leo turned and followed the bridge towards the East River.

Leo was in the flow of his running as the river came into view. The cold morning air already brought clarity to his mind. He crossed the road and gazed out over the river's broad, grey surface. Brooklyn was bleak and distant on the far side.

They didn't really have anything to prove that Andy was still even in the city. He could have travelled by train or bus anywhere in the country. Leo turned right and ran along the riverside. Traffic rumbled on raised highways above him. But, something made Leo doubt Andy would do that — he wouldn't just head off on his own. Andy wasn't a traveller. He liked to live in comfortable places.

After ten minutes battling against the icy wind rolling in from the river, Leo turned back into the city.

Andy wasn't a guy who could slip from place to place without being noticed. He just wasn't like that. Leo wished that they'd had some more in-depth conversations. He hardly knew his sister's husband. Leo thought about what it was like to talk to Andy. Andy constantly tried to belittle or patronise Leo. Andy would raise topics he knew Leo found awkward, or steer the conversation to paint himself as the cleverest or most successful person in the room.

Leo passed through a small city park and saw another runner, a slight black woman dressed in pink and running at an impressive pace. She skirted the park and started back in the direction from which she'd come. Leo thought of Allissa, still asleep in their hotel room.

Leo's phone vibrated in his pocket. He stopped running and slid it out. It was Niki Zadid.

"I think I have something for you." Niki cut straight to the point.

"Okay, what?" Leo said, his breath heavy.

"You okay?" Niki said.

"Yeah, I'm out running. What you got?"

"You must be crazy," Niki said. "I'll be back at the office in twenty. Meet there."

38

Niki Zadid rushed through the streets of Greenwich Village back towards her office. She was running late. It was going to be another busy day for one of New York's most discreet and, as such, sought after private detectives.

Niki had been up late the previous night on one case and had woken early to the relentless sound of her ringing phone. She would have been resentful of the intrusion if her clients didn't pay so well.

She rubbed the sleep from her eyes, straightened her headscarf and crossed the road between two forlorn, leafless trees.

Although Niki had a lot of work and it was well paid, it wasn't what she'd imagined the life of a Private Detective to be. She had pictured herself solving murders, tracking down missing people and reuniting families — not just profiting from the suspicions of husbands or wives. She frequently reminded herself that what she did was important. She was helping people with a problem. Yet, there was only so much sobbing into lavender-scented tissues or throwing expensive jewellery from the windows of her office that she could put up with.

It was all a repeating pattern — that was the real problem. Niki had been in business ten years, and in that time had seen several clients more than once. In one extreme case, a client had requested her help four times to investigate four different partners. These people met while married. They would coax each other from their husbands and wives into a new relationship, then, a few months later, suspect the new partner was doing it all over again. Sometimes they were, sometimes they weren't. That wasn't the point. If they couldn't find a trusting relationship, then maybe they just needed to spend some time on their own.

But, Niki reminded herself as she opened her office door, it paid well. She closed the door behind her and glanced around the room. A thick bar of winter sunlight shot through the large windows and glinted from the chandelier. The work paid very well.

People now knew her for this type of work. That was the problem. That was what her clients wanted. If she could just get one proper case, solve a crime, catch a killer or a thief, that would revamp her reputation.

"Play the news," Niki said. The smart speaker on the side table read out the headlines in its computerised voice. It seemed the NYPD were still no closer to catching the killer.

Now that was exactly the high-profile case Niki needed to solve. If she could get there before —

A buzz from the intercom interrupted her thoughts. She crossed the room and picked up the handset. An image of the two British detectives appeared on the screen.

"Yeah, come up," Niki said. "Stop," she shouted at the

smart speakers. The news report finished. "Play concentration playlist."

A deep thudding electronic bassline echoed through the room.

39

"We bought you coffee," Allissa said, holding out the cup as Niki opened the door. "You made it last time, so it was our turn. It's probably cold now, though."

Niki accepted the cup, thanked Allissa and sank into one of the large armchairs. She took a long sip. It was good, and without the pair knowing it, exactly as she liked it.

"You said you had news?" Leo took the chair opposite Niki.

"Yeah. I spoke to one of my contacts in the P.D. yesterday. They've got no trace of him yet."

Leo nodded. They'd heard nothing from the police either.

"So, I put a call into Axel —"

Niki's phone rang.

"Erin Kendall," she said, ending the call. "She's hired me to check up on her second sleazy husband. She thinks he'd been doing it with his ex-wife. He has."

"Who's Axel?" Leo asked.

"Let me explain." Niki uncrossed and then re-crossed

her legs. "New York's had a massive homeless problem since the great depression. To this day, more and more people arrive thinking the city holds the answers they need. There are around sixty-thousand homeless people in this city alone."

"Right, but how does that help —"

"That's sixty-thousand pairs of ears and eyes in every corner of the city," Niki said as she stood up. "There's one man who knows the right people to ask. He's a force to be reckoned with."

"Okay, let's give him a ring and see what he knows."

Niki turned and looked at Leo. "That's not the way Axel works. You've gotta go and see him if you want answers. I sent over a picture of your brother."

"Brother-in-law."

"Whatever. I sent over his picture yesterday, and Axel messaged today to say he's got news. So, we have to go and see him."

Niki eyed herself in the mirror, adjusted her headscarf and pulled on her camel trench coat.

"If anyone knows where your brother is," — Leo winced at the comment but didn't correct her — "then Axel's our guy."

Niki finished the last of the coffee and pulled open the door. "Come on, let's go."

40

He lay on his bed without moving and let the air slip from his lungs. Something about the way it tasted today excited him. Good and pure. It was as though he were truly alive for the first time. He could now see, think and feel more than ever before.

With his eyes still closed, he pictured the events of the previous night. His best one yet. First, she'd gone without too much of a fight — he liked that. He wanted to believe that on some level, his victims wanted their fate. They welcomed him to their bodies. She'd lain there in the alleyway, the blood running, silken and shimmering from her neck. Her glassy and expressionless eyes fixed on him.

He cut the dress from her quickly and saw her flawless body for the first time. Her supple skin begged for him to go to work on it. And, yes, he had gone to work. His best work yet.

His hands clenched beneath the bed covers. He pictured the blade moving through her skin. The canvas on which he'd formed his art.

His fingernails dug into the covers, and he gritted his teeth. She was so good. Maybe even perfect.

It was funny. He'd realised over the years that women found him attractive. Occasionally in the past, he'd taken them to bed. But that had never worked out as he'd wanted. He just wasn't really into it. Once or twice he'd made it work. But more often than not, he blamed the booze and went to sleep. But now, thinking of her skin exposed to the frigid night air, remembering the way the knife had pierced and sliced, he had no problem making things work. No problem at all.

He pulled another deep breath and rolled over.

Yes, something had now come alive, and he liked it very much.

41

"Axel!" Niki banged on a door between a second-hand clothes shop and a launderette. The only customer in either was a young Chinese man staring morosely at his spinning clothes.

"Axel!" Niki pounded the door again. The door shook against its fixings. Her strength and aggression surprised Leo.

They'd left Niki's office nearly an hour ago, walked across Greenwich Village, and got the metro over to Queens. Leo found the bubbling noise of the city disconcerting as he followed Niki through the metro station's crowds and back out into the bright, bitter morning.

"Axel!" Niki shouted yet again, followed by another staccato against the wood. Niki readied herself to pound for the fourth time. The door opened.

"What you want?" came a voice from the gap between the door and the frame. A young woman with bleary eyes appeared. She elongated the *want*, lending the question the tone of a stubborn teenager.

"Axel in?" Niki asked.

"Who you?" the woman demanded with no genuine conviction.

"We're friends." Niki pointed a thumb at Leo and Allissa standing behind her.

The woman's eyes flicked from Leo to Allissa, then back to Niki.

"Top of the stairs, first door on the right." She stood aside to let them pass.

Allissa smiled at the woman. She had long, mousy coloured hair and wore a baggy jumper with numerous holes.

The door at the top of the stairs opened before Niki reached it and a tiny man bounded out.

"Niki!" he shouted, smiling, his arms raised as though in praise. "It's good to see ya!"

Niki introduced Axel to Leo and Allissa, and they all shuffled inside.

"How have ya been?" Niki asked.

"Oh, you know," Axel replied, "getting by. Taking each day as it comes sorta thing."

Niki nodded.

"Sit down, sit down," Axel said, showing them his bedroom. Axel pointed Leo and Allissa towards his narrow bed. They sat down, and the bed creaked noisily. Niki perched on a box by the door and Axel leapt onto a small office chair in the corner.

"Niki got this place for me," Axel said with evident pride. "If it wasn't for her, I'd be out there somewhere. God knows where." His legs wiggled as he spoke. Even on the little chair, they hung without touching the floor. "We'd built it up all nice. It was a place just for us. Our own. Then the city wanted to take it back and turn it back into some kind of hotel. No one would help me, other than her. My angel."

"It wasn't really like that," Niki said. "I just pointed you in the right direction. You did most of the hard work yourselves."

"Nonsense, if we hadn't had your firm's backing —"

"I was a property lawyer at the time," Niki explained. "That must have been over fifteen years ago now. Axel contacted me, not knowing what to do. They couldn't pay the legals, so the city was just going to take this place."

"We ended up buying it for one dollar, and now it's ours." Axel waved his short arms to demonstrate the breadth of his kingdom.

"What're you doing here?" Niki pointed to the boxes strewn across the floor.

Axel straightened his bright yellow necktie.

"In these boxes," Axel said with grandeur, "are photos from thirty years of living in this and other squats around the city. From us first breaking in." He pulled a picture from a pile and showed Niki, Leo and Allissa. It was a gritty black and white print of an empty derelict room. "Renovating it." He produced another picture in which two men grinned towards the camera from a scaffold tower. "Oh, and this is my favourite." He reached for a photograph propped against a tin. "Before we went legal, we used to have gigs down where the shop now is. Bands would play just for their board. This is 'The Pistons'. Before they got big, obviously." In the picture, dark shapes swayed amongst the grains of black and white. "There's some from the day we officially became legal too," Axel continued. His leg wiggled with excitement. "There might even be one with you in it." He pointed at Niki.

"What're you doing with them?" Allissa asked.

Axel turned to her with a look of pantomime surprise.

"Why, cataloguing and digitising them, of course!" He

motioned to the dirty grey computer and scanner on the table beside him. A piece of masking tape covered the computer's built-in webcam.

"This is an important record of social history," Axel said. "This is our history. Galleries across the world would be interested in this."

"These photos are great," Niki said, flicking through a pile.

"I know," Axel said. "This is my life's work, and now this place is secure, I can concentrate on telling my story. But you didn't come here to talk about that!" Axel said abruptly. He turned to face Leo and Allissa.

"We're looking for his brother," Niki said, nodding at Leo.

"Brother-in-law," Leo interjected.

"Yes, yes, the picture you sent." Axel took a pair of thick-rimmed glasses from his breast pocket and slid them on. Then he picked up a large mobile phone from beside the computer. "Now, where is he?" he muttered, scrolling through the phone. "Ah yes, he's been seen. Or at least my man thought it was him from the picture you sent."

"Where?" Leo asked.

"That's interesting," Axel said, ignoring Leo and tapping his chin. "They saw him twice. Niki honey, pass me that map there." He pointed to a shelf above Niki's head.

Niki passed Axel the rolled-up map. Axel hopped down from his seat and spread it across the floor. Niki shuffled her box backwards to make space. It was a map of Manhattan, covered in markings of various colours.

"Look, here we are. Let's see." Axel glanced back at his phone and then down to the map. "Right, so yesterday he was here." Axel jabbed a stubby finger at a corner in central Manhattan. "He spent the night there apparently, left at some point in the early evening. Evidently, he pissed a few people off. He was shouting all night."

Leo thought that sounded familiar. His eyes narrowed.

"What is that place?" Allissa dug out her phone and took notes.

"It's part of the bus station, but that level's been out of use for years. A lot of our guys go there in the evenings when it's cold. And then he was seen,"— Axel checked the details on the phone again — "yes, that's right. Going into Madison's Corner Café."

Leo looked down in disbelief. Although it would be incredible if this man really had a lead on Andy, Leo wasn't hopeful.

Niki sat with her legs crossed and her back straight. So far, she seemed like a skilful detective. If she believed Axel, then maybe there was some truth in it.

Axel poked the map with a finger. "Right there," he said. "Last night, your brother was right there."

42

Andy woke up with a start. Visions of a crumpled car, metal crunching against concrete, and a man dressed as a cowboy spun through his mind. He swallowed. His mouth was thick with the taste of tequila and the dozen other drinks he'd consumed the night before. He opened his eyes cautiously. He was in a room. That was good. With no recollection of where he was, he'd half expected to be out on the street somewhere.

It had been a fun night, though. He smiled to himself. The cowboy. The jazz club. The bottle of tequila. He couldn't remember leaving, but by some miracle had found himself a bed. Not just a bed, but a room, too. Andy peered around happily. Sachets of tea and coffee stood to attention on a small table in the corner, and a bathroom sat in gloom through a door to his right.

Maybe Otto had brought him here. Maybe he'd found it himself. Either way, that was good. It meant he didn't need to face up to things just yet.

Andy still wasn't sure what it was he had to face up to, though. A snagging worry took hold. He didn't even know why he was in New York. He didn't live here. At least, it didn't seem familiar.

Andy shoved the thoughts away and told himself not to think about it. There would be time to worry about things like that. Today, he wanted to enjoy himself.

Andy stood up and stretched. The flowery bedsheets were still made, meaning he'd failed to make it into the bed properly. The floral motif continued throughout the room. The wallpaper, the curtains and even the dusty paintings all contained flowers. This was a very cheap hotel.

Still, it was better than where he'd slept the night before.

Andy grabbed his trousers from the floor and rummaged through the pockets. He pulled out two crumpled ten dollar bills and a load of coins.

Shit.

He must have spent, or lost, almost all his money. He could probably afford one more drink, though. That's what he needed. Before things started to feel real.

Andy crossed to the bathroom and stepped into the shower. He stood beneath the water for ages, fighting off the negative thoughts which tried to encroach his mind. Something bad had happened. But what?

Andy forced the thoughts away. He needed to get a drink. That would stop his mind whirring like this. He stepped out of the shower and searched for a toothbrush. There wasn't one. He scooped up some water and swilled it around his teeth. He would have to get a toothbrush later, too. Andy glanced at himself in the mirror. He looked pale.

The old-fashioned phone on the bedside table rang. Its shrill noise startled Andy. He lumbered across the room and answered it.

"Andy Harris?" A distant voice reverberated through the ancient handset.

"Yeah, that's me."

"It's the lobby. Can you please come down? There's something I need to discuss with you."

Andy dressed quickly and descended three flights of stairs to the reception area. The swirling floral theme continued through the building. He padded over the sticky carpet towards the reception area and froze. A pair of police officers stood at the desk.

Andy stepped behind the wall and peered out at them. They were talking with the receptionist. Andy was too far away to make out what they were saying. Andy's heart hammered against his chest. They were after him. They had to be.

Andy glanced around. To his right, the police officers spoke with the receptionist. To his left, double doors led out into the street. He looked from one to the other. Andy wasn't ready to face up to whatever was going on yet. He turned and stepped out into the winter afternoon.

Thick grey clouds strained the winter light from the sky. Premature darkness settled across the city. Only wearing a shirt and a thin jacket, Andy felt a chill. He would need to get something warmer before the evening arrived. That would be a problem with his limited money.

He glanced back at the hotel and wondered why he'd run. It seemed like the right thing to do at the time. But even now, just thirty seconds away from the door, he wasn't so sure. He would deal with whatever was wrong tomorrow, maybe. Today he wanted to be on his own.

He angled his face away from the sky in a vain attempt to avoid the drizzling rain and walked hurriedly away. He'd feel much better after a beer. He just didn't want to face up to anything right now. All he wanted to do was find another bar and drink some more.

Andy paused at an intersection. An army of people pushed this way and that, all wrapped up against the winter chill. A man carrying an umbrella pushed Andy aside. A drop of rain slid down Andy's neck and he shuddered.

Andy turned onto a quieter street and walked in close to the buildings. He could stay drier here without the torrents of people pushing past. He glanced up at the brooding sky. The thick wet rag of clouds choked the top of the surrounding towers now. Andy turned up the collar of his jacket and hunched his shoulders. He skirted a stream of water, splashing onto the pavement from a metal fire escape.

Andy paused outside a pub and peered in through the steamed-up windows. A dozen men drank at the bar. Andy salivated, imagining the hedonistic buzz of alcohol. He rummaged through his pocket and pulled out the crumpled notes. He smiled and stepped inside. Everything would all feel better after a beer or two.

43

Leo and Allissa stepped into the cavernous interior of Madison's Corner Café. Sport and news played on half a dozen giant plasma screens, the beer taps sparkled, and a spectrum of bottles gleamed from the back bar. The air conditioner kicked out hot air and hits of the nineties bellowed from the speakers.

Allissa crossed to a pair of stools at the bar and settled into one. Leo followed.

"We might as well have a beer, to blend in, you know?" She scrutinised the taps.

"Just the one," Leo conceded. It was still early in the afternoon, and there was no telling how the day might play out. Leo knew from experience that investigations were unpredictable.

"Get you a drink?" said the barman, smiling from Allissa to Leo.

"Sure," Allissa said, returning his smile and ordering two pints of Brooklyn Lager.

Leo examined the place as the barman poured their drinks. This was probably a dead end. There was no way

Andy could have come for a casual drink after a near-fatal car wreck. It just wasn't possible.

"We've just got to see what turns up," Allissa said, reading Leo's expression. "I know it seems mad that he would've come in here after the crash, you know. But we'll try it."

"Yeah, you're right. Things never turn out how we expect." Their previous cases had proved that beyond any doubt.

"It's not an awful place to hang out for a couple of hours either," Allissa said, thanking the barman for the beers and lifting hers to her lips.

Leo gazed at the giant TV screens behind the bar. Four played sports, which he couldn't name, let alone understand. Two more played news. The news channel's icon swirled and spun across the screen. The graphics faded, and a broad-shouldered anchor-man appeared. 'Victim number three for The Downtown Ripper' slid from across the bottom of the screen as the newsman read the story.

The report cut to a shot of the crime scene. Yellow tape fluttered around an alleyway, and police officers stood beside a crime scene preservation tent.

"Leo, hello?"

"Sorry, was just watching that." He pointed at the screen. "It looks pretty bad. That's three people this guy's now killed."

The camera zoomed out to reveal the diner beside which the body had been found.

Allissa looked from the screen to the barman. He caught her eye and smiled back.

The news report rolled onto the next story. A man wearing white gloves held a gun, and a flag flew at half-mast.

"Tell you what," Allissa said. "You go outside and give Emma a ring. I'll have a chat with the barman and see if he remembers Andy being in here last night."

"Sure," Leo agreed, taking another sip of the beer. He slid off the barstool, rummaged through his pockets for his phone, and headed out to the street.

"I wonder if you can help me with something," Allissa probed. The barman approached. "We're looking for a friend of ours. We think he was in here last night. Were you working last night?"

"I was, yeah," the barman said, leaning in towards Allissa.

Allissa pulled up a photo of Andy on her phone.

"We think he was here, but we're not sure. Do you remember him?"

The barman examined the photograph.

Allissa watched his reaction closely, waiting for him to shake his head. This lead was tenuous at best.

"Yeah. Yeah, I do," the barman said, pointing at the picture.

"Wait, what?"

The barman leaned in further. "Yeah, I'm pretty sure of it. He came in on his own. Then he ended up drinking with Otto, one of our regulars. I think they left together."

Allissa examined the man in disbelief. Axel might have got this right.

"Okay," she said, concentrating. "Okay. Did you notice anything strange about him?"

"No, not really. Just a normal guy."

"Do you remember what he was wearing?"

"Nah, not really, shirt and jeans maybe."

"How do we find this guy he was chatting to? Otto?"

The door clattered open, and a blast of cold air streamed

in from the street. Allissa glanced across, assuming Leo had finished on the phone. A large man wearing jeans, a red shirt and a wide-brimmed Stetson lumbered into the bar. The steel heels of his boots clacked across the wooden floor.

"That's your man right there." The barman pointed at the new arrival. "Regular as clockwork."

44

Allissa watched the man lumber through the bar. He was well over six-feet tall and as wide as two men. His body swayed as though relying on centrifugal force to prevent him from falling over. He reached for a bar stool and slid onto it.

"Excuse me," the barman said to Allissa as he walked across to the new arrival.

Leo pushed through the door and re-took his seat beside Allissa.

"How's Emma?" Allissa asked.

"Yeah, okay. Going out of her mind with worry."

"Have the police told them anymore?"

Leo shook his head.

The barman poured tequila and orange juice over crushed ice in a tall glass.

"Well, I've got some interesting news. You'll never guess what?" Leo stared at her. "Andy was here last night. The barman saw him. And, he was drinking with that man." Allissa pointed at the cowboy.

"Seriously?" Leo said. "That guy Niki took us to see wasn't just making things up?"

"It seems not. They left together too, apparently."

"You spoke to him yet?"

"That's what we're going to do right now," Allissa turned to the barman, who added a teaspoon of tabasco to an orange-coloured drink. "What's he drinking?"

"Tequila sunrise," the barman replied. "Well, it's Otto's version of it, anyway. He can't get enough of them."

"We'll buy him that one. Add it to our tab." Allissa turned to Leo. "Come on. Let's find out what happened last night."

Allissa picked up her pint and walked towards the cowboy.

"Hi there. Otto, isn't it?" Allissa said. "I need your help with something."

The wide-brimmed hat cast a shadow across Otto's face. He turned to face Allissa.

"We're looking for the guy you were with in here last night. It's his brother-in-law." Allissa pointed at Leo.

"This one's on them," the barman said, putting Otto's drink in front of him.

Otto nodded, picked up the glass with a hand the size of a frying pan and downed a third of it. He wiped his lips, then considered Allissa and Leo through narrowed eyes. His grizzled face sagged in the dim overhead light.

"Yeah, who's that?" he said, licking his lips. His voice had a Texan twang.

"A guy called Andy," Leo said. "You were drinking in here with him last night."

Otto nodded. Leo dug out his phone, found the picture of Andy and showed it to Otto.

Otto's mouth tensed and he nodded again.

"Hey, you cops?" Otto barked, taking another greedy sip of the drink.

"No," Allissa said. "We're missing persons investigators. We're trying to track down that man."

"Do you want another one of those," Leo asked, pointing at the glass. Maybe they'd get more out of this guy if they loosened him up first.

"Sure," Otto said, gazing at the glass. "If you're sure you're not cops. I ain't done nuthin' to talk to cops about."

"We're definitely not," Allissa said.

"Well, okay." Otto's face cracked into a smile. "Say, if you're not cops, then you have one of these too." He pointed at the glass.

"Sure," Leo said. He nodded to the barman and ordered one regular and two non-alcoholic tequila sunrises.

"What y'all wanna know then?"

"We're looking for this guy." Allissa showed Otto the picture again. "Did you see him last night?"

Otto wrapped a giant hand around his chin and examined the picture.

"Yeah," he said. "He was in here yesterday. We were drinking together."

"Did he come in on his own?" Allissa asked.

"Yeah, he was on his own, then we got chatting at the bar. We had a few drinks together. He seemed like an alright guy. Why're you looking for him?" Otto's expression darkened.

"He's left his wife and son without telling them where he was going," Allissa said.

Otto nodded again. The round of drinks arrived. Otto took a greedy sip.

"You left here together?" Allissa asked.

Otto thought for a moment. "Yeah, we went to Opus. I go there every night. It's a cool place."

Otto rubbed his nose, sniffed, and drank some more. The glass was already half empty.

"Do you remember what you talked about?" Allissa asked.

Otto looked confused.

"With Andy last night? Do you remember what you spoke about?"

Otto drained his glass, waved the barman over and ordered another.

"Yeah. Just the usual stuff. He was visiting New York. Actually, no, that was interesting. He said he couldn't remember why he was here. It was pretty funny. I think he'd had a bit too much of something or other." Otto dabbed his nose.

"He didn't know where he was?" Leo asked.

Otto picked up the empty glass and tried to take a swig from it. Leo doubted these drinks were his first of the day.

"No, he knew he was in New York, but he couldn't remember why. He said he was sure he'd figure it out before too long. Sounded crazy, but we get all sorts in this city. He was a good guy. From England. Where're you guys from?"

"We're from England too," Leo said. "Did he seem okay? You know, did he seem injured or hurt or confused?"

Otto chewed over an answer.

"Was he in a good mood?" Leo asked.

"Yeah, I think so. He was good. He didn't seem injured. Just like a normal guy. Good drinker, too. We had shots. Yeah, we need to have some shots."

Otto pointed a thick finger and Leo and Allissa.

"No, we're —"

"If you're not cops, then you need to have shots." Otto jabbed his finger. "Cops wouldn't do shots."

The barman delivered the tequila sunrise, and Otto ordered a round of shots.

"So, at the next place, the Opus club? What happened there?" Allissa said.

Otto seemed to have one sip, two sip or three sip answers to questions. This was definitely a three-sip answer. Otto thought so hard that he almost emptied the glass.

"I don't remember," Otto said finally. Shots arrived on a wooden board, and Otto distributed them with surprising dexterity.

"Nah, I can't remember," Otto said. "It was late by then. We went to the Opus. Hey, do you reckon he'll come back tonight? He was a good guy."

Otto picked up one of the oily shot glasses and eyed Leo and Allissa until they did the same.

Leo felt a wave of nausea when the liquid hit his stomach. He hated tequila.

"How did you and Andy get there?" Allissa asked.

"Taxi," Otto said. "It's not far."

"Where's the club?" Leo asked. "I mean, what street's it on?"

"No point telling you," Otto said, "they wouldn't let you in."

Otto held his glass in the air to signal for the barman to fetch him another.

"I can help you, though," Otto declared.

"How?" Allissa asked.

"You can come with me tonight."

45

He eyed himself in the mirror and smiled. The person who smiled back at him was good, but not perfect. He leaned in to get a closer look. His skin glowed the way he liked it. His expensive skincare routine made sure of that. He clenched his teeth and parted his lips. His super-white teeth shone. There was nothing wrong there.

He stood up straight and flattened the collar of his tailored, crisp white shirt that hung from his body in just the way he liked. Everything looked good, but just not right. His grey eyes gazed back at him, slow and sombre. Dull and morbid. That was it. He felt drained after the excitement of the last two nights. He would come alive later, when he stood amid the baying crowd of New York's elite, picking his target like a prized pig at a meat market.

That's when the fun would start — selecting his target, persuading her to come with him, and then having his fun.

Tonight, as per tradition, he would lead her down to Washington Square.

His hand shifted to the knife concealed beneath his trousers. Its rigid shape was a promise of the action to come.

He gazed at himself in the mirror now. His eyes radiated mysteriously. That was it, he thought, that was what he needed.

He pulled on a jacket, tucked the bracelet beneath his cuff and crossed to the door.

The fun was about to start.

46

"Mr Otto," the doorman said, pulling the velvet rope aside. "Good to see you again. I wasn't sure you were going to make it in this weather. They say they're expecting snow."

Otto looked at the man. Both were of a similar height, although the doorman outdid Otto with his bulging muscles.

"It'll take more than the threat of snow to keep me away," Otto said. "I've been drinking in this city in worse winters than this."

"You've got some more guests tonight?" The doorman stared down his crooked nose at Leo and Allissa.

"Something like that." Otto lumbered passed the doorman and descended the stairs heavily.

"You let them in, so why can't we just go in? It's raining!" moaned a woman at the front of the queue. Allissa glanced at her, shivering against the evening's chill in her bright dress and thin jacket. The doorman crossed his arms over an expansive chest and gazed down at the woman. Allissa

New York

couldn't help but feel sorry for anyone out in the rain tonight. That was one reason she rarely went to clubs. It all seemed like a lot of effort for ear-splitting music and overpriced drinks. A simple pub any day, that was her thing. The dingier the better.

The taxi journey from Madison's Café to the Opus Jazz Club had been quick. The streets were quiet, dark and wet.

Allissa followed Leo and Otto down a stairway lit in shades of pink and blue. A twanging double bass beat from somewhere beneath them. A small man in a suit held open the door at the bottom of the stairs. Allissa thanked him as she stepped into the club. The blue and pink lighting continued throughout the elegant and exclusive venue. The dancefloor in the centre was full of people moving to the beat.

"Your usual booth?" the man holding the door said to Otto.

Otto nodded, and the man led them across the club.

"Another bottle?" the man said. Otto nodded again.

"You come here every night?" Allissa asked, shuffling into the booth.

"Yeah," Otto replied, his eyes drifting around the room.

"Where did you and Andy sit?" Allissa said.

"Right here," Otto replied. "This is my seat. I always sit here."

The man returned with drinks. First, he placed an unopened bottle of tequila on the table, followed by three glasses.

Leo's throat felt sticky. He couldn't drink any more of this.

"Would you like anything else?" the waiter asked, turning to Leo and Allissa.

Otto uncapped the bottle and poured a considerable measure of tequila into each glass.

"We'll come up to the bar and have a look," Allissa said.

Otto kicked back one shot and immediately poured himself another. Allissa doubted he would be any more use to them tonight.

47

He stepped out of the taxi and glanced around. A group of bedraggled people queued outside the jazz club's door. The streets were quiet tonight. Most of the city had stayed at home to shelter from the rain and the cold. He was confident that it wouldn't make a difference to him. It wouldn't matter. He would still find someone. He only needed one.

Of course, his great-grandfather didn't have these problems. People were always out in those days. They had nowhere else to go. They littered the streets, just begging for someone to help them towards a cold and welcoming grave. He smiled at the thought.

"Good evening sir." The doorman recognised him and moved the rope aside.

He nodded and glanced at the queue. That's where the silver, shimmering dress had first caught his attention last night. He'd decided there and then that he wanted her. He'd decided that he would have her. And, as usual, he got what he wanted.

She was so good. So supple. Just perfect.

Descending the stairs towards the nightclub, the warm air and babbling music rising to greet him, he felt the knife concealed beneath his trousers.

This was it. This was the hunt. This was what he lived for. He was the predator, and this was his game.

The air bristled with the thud of the double bass and citrus tang of cocktails. He paused at the bottom of the stairs and drank it in.

He had never heard of the band playing tonight, The Kat Trio. People came to the Opus Jazz Club to see world class musicians. They came in all weathers, any night of the week, and paid a lot of money for the pleasure.

He didn't pay. He was too well connected for that. People wanted him to visit their clubs. It was an honour for them, he supposed.

He reached the bottom of the stairs, and the door opened. He stepped inside. The place was busy, as usual. It was always busier than the club's humble frontage suggested.

Drinkers lounged in booths along the far wall, and a small crowd of dancers twisted across the floor. The sensible early-evening crowd of jazz aficionados would have left already, and the music thumped for the late-night party-goers.

A flurry of laughter echoed from a group of girls in a booth at the back. Three prosecco bottles sat belly up in a freestanding ice bucket — their night was a heavy one. They were the ones to watch.

He turned to look at the band. Three men swung, strummed and pounded on a piano, a double bass, and drums. The music did nothing for him. It was at best an irritant he could do without. But, like the watering hole that brought the prey to the lion, it delivered him what he wanted.

A group of young men gesticulated drunkenly in the next booth. One banged on the table while another lolled back into the seat. He would leave them well alone.

"Welcome, sir. Where would you like to sit today?" The host's eyes sparkled beneath the muted pink of the club's lighting. "At the bar again, like last night?"

"Yes, yes, please."

It was a bold move to return to the scene of the crime straight away. Maybe it was even foolish. The police could have asked around. Whilst he knew there was no CCTV inside the club, one of the staff may have seen him talking to her. Although they didn't leave together — he was careful of that — someone could have noticed their similar departure times.

It was a risk, but it was minimal and well worth it.

He examined the host's expression for any twitch of suspicion. There wasn't even the slightest shimmer of mistrust in the man's rodent-like features.

The host led him to a leather-topped stool at the end of the bar. Two young men sat beside him, deep in conversation. Their well-cut suits and glassy eyes the result of drinking since the office closed. They would cause him no trouble. They probably wouldn't even notice he was there.

"Thank you," he said, sitting down and resting his elbow on the bar. He liked this seat. It was easy to order drinks, and more importantly, offered a superb view of the club. He spun around to face the room.

The band played seamlessly into the next song, and the stomping of the crowd intensified.

"Can I get you a drink, sir?"

He ordered a beer and a glass of water.

Excitement tingled his fingers. This was it. This was why he did it. This was what he wanted.

48

"Andy hardly knows the city, so there's a good chance he'll come back here. It'll be comfortable and friendly to him," Allissa said, thinking out loud.

"Yeah. I think that's exactly what he'd do," Leo said. "He's not used to big cities or new places either, so I think he'll be drawn towards something familiar."

Leo and Allissa stood at the bar. Leo ordered two beers and turned to face Allissa. A beer was acceptable, but multiple shots of Otto's tequila would never end well. Allissa's eyes shone beneath the club's pink and blue lighting. Leo remembered them dancing at the street party in St Lucia just days ago.

"The problem is, will he be able to get in without Otto?" Leo said, watching a small crowd stare around the club excitedly. The Opus was obviously a big deal.

"Good point." Allissa gave a note to the barman. "We'll have to wait and see."

The barman put two bottled beers on the bar.

"But we might also find someone else who was here last night."

Leo agreed, taking a sip of his beer.

"You keep Otto talking." Allissa pointed at Otto slumped in the booth. "See if you can get him to remember anything else. I'll ask around."

Leo nodded, and made his way back to the booth. Otto poured himself another shot. Leo didn't know how the guy sustained so much booze.

Allissa searched the club. Despite the noise of the music, the drinking and the dancing, the place was comfortable. It was unlike the boisterous, chaotic clubs she'd reluctantly been to over the years.

An uproar of laughter echoed from a group of men. Allissa glanced at them. They wore crisp shirts and the glazed expression of immature drinkers. She turned to watch the group who'd just arrived greet some friends on the dancefloor before heading to the bar.

What Allissa needed was to speak to one of the staff. They may have been working last night and could have seen Andy. Three people worked the bar, frantically making cocktails and pouring drinks, whilst the man who'd greeted them took orders from the booths.

"Hey, how are you?"

Allissa assumed the voice wasn't talking to her and continued to watch the crowd. A hand touched her on the arm. She stopped, turned, and stared into the deep grey eyes of the man beside her.

49

Niki took the stairs slowly, fumbled with the key and clattered through her apartment door. She tapped at the wall until she found the light switch. Even though she'd lived in the place for years, she spent so little time here, that coming home always felt alien. Often she was so tired from long hours tailing someone, that she fell straight into the sleep of necessity on the sofa.

She slid out of her trench coat and hung it on the hook by the door. Then she took off her headscarf, pulled out the band securing her hair and shook it free. Her hair tumbled across her shoulders and down her back. She ran her fingers through it and crossed to the sofa. She slumped into the cushions, took off her shoes and checked the time. Three a.m. That was an early night by her standards. Sometimes she'd be awake until daylight following some cheating husband or deceitful wife.

Niki gazed out at the night sky through the window and wondered, as she often did, why people were so dishonest to one another. It wasn't as though they'd been forced into marrying. They entered into it willingly, and yet spent so much time and money deceiving each other.

This case was slightly different, though. She dug out her phone and scrolled through the pictures. She'd followed Karl Everdeen on the request of his wife for two weeks now, and found him doing nothing wrong. On every occasion, he went where he had said he was going to.

Niki stretched and yawned. At least there was some honesty left in the city.

Somewhere nearby a metro train rattled.

Niki's apartment was small compared to the grandeur of her office. It was just three rooms above a convenience store, but she liked it. She still remembered the day they'd moved in. Newly married and looking forward to their lives together. Her eyes darted to the small picture on the cluttered writing desk. She couldn't see the photograph clearly, but that didn't matter. Time had seared the image into her mind's eye. Hassan and Niki, on their honeymoon in Paris, the Eiffel Tower looming in the misty morning light behind them. They're laughing in the photograph, exhilarated by the new city, the early morning air, and the start of their lives together.

Niki pushed her hands across her face and exhaled. She needed to sleep. Tiredness made her emotional, and emotions had no place in her line of work. Placing her hands on her knees and ignoring the gems which now sparkled from the corners of her eyes, Niki stood. That was the past, and no amount of wishing, hoping or praying could bring that back.

50

"Are you looking for someone?" the man at the bar asked Allissa. Allissa hadn't noticed him before. Probably in his early thirties, he had a wide exuberant smile and a comma of thick brown hair. There was something about him that Allissa recognised, though she couldn't work out what it was.

"Yes, sort of." She took a sip of her beer. "I want to talk to someone about a friend of mine. He was in here last night."

The man's expression didn't change.

"Were you here last night?" Allissa asked.

The man's eyes flicked to the left. Allissa noticed the gesture but didn't understand it. A calm smile broke across his face. His teeth shone iridescent beneath the bar's colourful lights.

"Yes, I was, actually," he said. "I work just around the corner. I often work late and come down for a drink or two when I finally finish."

"Fantastic," Allissa said, hardly believing her luck. "We're searching for a guy called Andy. If you were here, you might be able to help." She dug out her phone. "We know he was in here, but we need to know if he spoke with, or left with anyone."

"I getcha. Sure. Anything I can do to help." The man took a swig of his beer. "You don't sound like you're from around here?" He flashed a sparkling smile at Allissa.

"No, we're missing person's investigators." Allissa smiled in return. "Just here on this case."

"Oh, cool. What a great job. Do you travel a lot?"

"Let me show you a picture of the guy we're looking for." Allissa steered the conversation back to the case and showed him the picture of Andy. "Did you see him in here last night?"

The man leaned in and stared at the photograph for a few seconds. Allissa watched his expression. He showed no signs of recognition.

"I don't think I remember him." He shook his head. "Nothing jumps out, anyway."

"Okay, no problem," Allissa said. "Do you recognise anyone else here now who was also here last night?"

The man gazed around the bar. "I can't see anyone I recognise, but I'll keep looking. Do you want another one of those while I'm thinking about it?" He pointed towards the bottle in Allissa's hand. "If you're allowed to drink on the job, that is." The shining smile lit up his face again.

"I'm good thanks," Allissa told him.

"I can see that's almost empty. You don't even have to talk to me while you drink it if you don't want to." He got the barman's attention and ordered two more beers.

Allissa glanced over at Leo, trying to talk to Otto. The wide-brimmed hat had sunk even lower over the cowboy's face.

"Here ya go."

Allissa took the bottle reluctantly and sensed the pang of recognition again. She was sure she'd seen this man before, although she couldn't work out where.

"I'm sorry I've not introduced myself." The man offered his hand. "My name's Seth Stryker. That was so rude of me."

Allissa accepted the proffered hand. His grip was firm, and his skin soft.

"I run a true crime blog," Seth said. "This last week's been pretty crazy with this killer all over the news."

Allissa's eyes narrowed as a realisation dawned.

"That's where I recognise you from!" Allissa said, pointing at him. "You were on the telly the other night, right?"

"That's right," Seth nodded. "The news stations get me to comment when they have nothing else to go on. It's not that I know much more than anybody else, but they like the story."

"Does that happen often?" Allissa asked.

"More than you'd think. There are so many news stations with hours to fill. They always want someone to comment on a crime."

"How do you know what to say if the police aren't releasing the story?" Allissa said.

"They love it when I compare the case to previous historical crimes. That's what my website's all about. History's greatest criminals and how they got away with it."

Allissa took a swig of the beer.

"It's grown out of all proportion really," Seth said. "I didn't think it would get this big when I started. I didn't do it to get rich or anything. I just wrote about interesting things."

"You must have lots of readers."

"Yeah," Seth said, "a few million a year. People are just intrigued, I think. And I thought I was the only one!"

"You must know a lot about what's happening in the city?" Allissa said.

"Yeah, I keep up with the news. There's always something dark and dangerous going on in New York."

51

"Do you recognise anyone who was also here last night?" Leo asked.

Otto mumbled something inaudible. Talking was beyond the man's capabilities now. That wasn't surprising considering the half-empty bottle of tequila on the table.

"Otto?" Leo said, trying to catch the man's bloodshot eye. *Could eyes that bloodshot even work?* "Anything you can tell me about what happened last night would be really helpful."

"Last night?" Otto said. "What happened last night?"

"You know, you were here with Andy, that guy I showed you. You were telling us about him. You came here together."

"Who's that?" Otto said, sitting up straight and pouring himself another drink.

"The guy you were here with last night."

"Last night?"

Leo sighed. The conversation had been going round in circles for the last few minutes. He wouldn't get anything useful from Otto now. Leo glanced across the room. Allissa was talking to a man at the bar. Leo hoped her conversation was proving more useful than his.

The man bought two bottles of beer and passed one to Allissa. He smiled, and his exceptionally white teeth shone like the battalion of bottles on the back-bar.

Allissa swigged the beer as the man spoke. She nodded and smiled in reply. Allissa appeared to be enjoying the conversation. Jealousy bubbled through him.

When running away from killers in Kathmandu, or on the trail of kidnappers in Hong Kong, things between Leo and Allissa had been simple. Leo had been searching for Mya then, so he and Allissa could only be friends. Now that he'd put that to rest, something new simmered beneath their relationship.

Otto pushed a glass of tequila across the table towards Leo.

Leo rejected it and stood. He felt a mood of despair descend across him. Andy wasn't here. They weren't getting any closer to finding him, and now they were wasting time. If Andy was going to arrive, he would be here by now. They couldn't stay all night waiting for him.

Leo finished his beer and pushed through the club towards Allissa.

"This is my partner, my business partner, Leo," Allissa said as Leo approached.

"Hi, Leo." The man offered Leo his hand. "Allissa's been telling me all about your case here. It sounds like you guys are making some excellent progress."

"Yeah, we're getting there." Leo nodded. He turned to Allissa. "We should get off. We've got a lot more to do tomorrow."

"Sure. Yes, you're right. Seth, take my number and if you think of anything useful, please get in touch."

"Will do, sure," Seth said, his smile unfaltering. Allissa read out her number, and Seth entered it into his phone.

Leo wriggled into his coat, scowling.

"I'll send you over that picture of Andy," Allissa said. "If you see him, or if you think of anything —"

"I'll get in touch." Seth leaned in and kissed Allissa on the cheek. "Allissa, it's been great to meet you. You too, Leo."

"Thanks. See you," Allissa said, following Leo towards the exit.

Seth took a swig from his beer. His grey eyes didn't leave Allissa's figure until she'd disappeared up the stairs.

52

"He's a fascinating guy," Allissa said, turning as they climbed the stairs. "Remember, we saw him on TV at Niki's place?"

"What, that was him?" Leo said.

"Yeah, he runs a true crime blog. The news stations interview him when they don't have much to go on. He talks about how the case relates to historical criminals. He was in the club last night too, but he says he didn't see Andy."

"That doesn't mean Andy wasn't there," Leo said, stepping out onto the pavement. It was still raining, and the night was quiet. Two or three people shuffled past with umbrellas. Music thumped from a passing car.

"No, of course not," Allissa said, watching a figure stagger through a patch of light further down the street. There was something familiar about him.

"Good idea," Leo said absentmindedly. He raised his hand as the green 'For Hire' light of a taxi slid their way.

"Is that —" Allissa began, staring at the retreating figure.

"Taxi," Leo shouted. "Chinatown, please."

The figure disappeared into a side street.

"No, it couldn't be," Allissa muttered, then followed Leo into the taxi.

53

This way he could see her before he committed. He could see her closely. The clothes women wore to nightclubs like this didn't leave much to the imagination. He could examine every inch of her body — above her clothes, anyway. He'd get to know what hid beneath intimately later.

But there was more to it than that. He could see how she acted with her friends. How she smiled and laughed and how easily he could draw her away. He found it strange that a young and beautiful woman would choose to spend a night with a stranger, as opposed to her friends.

It reminded him of a childhood visit to a great-uncle's dilapidated house on the outskirts of some once-exclusive neighbourhood. In the garden stood a tree, overrun with ivy. The tree was being suffocated by it, killed by the creeper which strangled every inch of its bark. He remembered thinking that when the tree fell, the ivy would fall too. It was as though the ivy worked towards its own demise.

Maybe that's what she wanted. She knew the risks. Maybe playing close to them was the ultimate excitement.

The supreme frivolous pleasure. Perhaps he fulfilled some part of her desire too.

There it was — the lingering of her eyes from the dancefloor.

He observed her coolly and lifted the beer to his lips. She was beautiful. A dress of iridescent blue clung to her body. It swung and shimmered. He examined her back, the bulge of her bum and the impossible slenderness of her legs.

He turned and ordered another beer. She would come to him. She knew the danger. She, just like him, chased the ultimate thrill — pursued a supreme high which tonight, he hoped, would be her last.

54

Andy stumbled through the night. The rain poured across his face. His shoulders slumped, and his head lolled. He didn't bother trying to remain dry now. The rain pounded across him. It chilled him to the core. Thunder hammered across the sky.

Andy glanced upwards and then slid a bottle of whiskey from his jacket pocket, unscrewed the cap and took a swig. The alcohol warmed his throat and stomach. He could fight off the cold with drink alone. He glanced at the bottle, it was almost empty.

Andy couldn't remember why he'd run from the hotel this morning. He couldn't understand it. If he'd just stayed there, the police would have explained everything to him. Then none of this would have happened. They knew why he was here. They were just trying to help him understand what he'd forgotten. But, instead of taking that chance, he'd run like a coward. Perhaps that's what he was: a coward who ran from everything difficult or scary.

Andy reached an intersection and stopped. Warm lights from an apartment shone into the street.

Whatever Andy was doing here, he had to be staying somewhere. He would have an apartment, or a hotel room, or something.

Andy pushed the heels of his hands into his face. He just couldn't remember. Did he live here? Who did he live with? He had some vague recollections of a house which he assumed was home. But it was a house, not an apartment — that he remembered for sure. And there was a woman — he was sure of that, too. Was she his wife? His girlfriend? The ghosts of memories fled from his mind.

The traffic light above the intersection flickered from red to green. Two cars swished past. Spray from their tyres spattered Andy's trousers.

The inky expanse of a city park spread out across the road. The towers of downtown blinked like grey ghosts in the thick sky beyond.

A large stone arch extended across the park's entrance. Andy gazed up at it. At least beneath there he could stay dry.

55

"Don't you dance?" came a voice from behind him. He knew its owner already. He pictured her. The shimmering blue dress. The cascading long blonde hair. The gleaming smile.

He took a sip from the bottle and turned. The temperature in the room had risen in the last hour. A humid haze pumped through the air.

Of course he danced. He danced every night. Just not the dancing that involved music and nightclubs.

He smiled. His grey eyes glistened. "I prefer to watch. You're all doing such a good job that... " He let his voice trail off.

She considered him.

He planned to speak in riddles. He'd keep her focused and guessing.

Her smile reappeared. "I'm Maisie," she said, offering him a hand.

He accepted it, introduced himself and kissed her on the cheek. She smelled good. Yes, she smelled very good. He pulled a deep breath, his eyes half-closed. This was it.

New York

"If you don't dance," — she rested an elbow on the bar — "what do you come here for?"

A good question, he thought.

"You know," he said, raising his bottle of beer, "just to unwind after the day. Do you want one, by the way?" He raised the drink.

"Sure." She selected something from the menu.

He smirked at the cost. *Well, okay,* he thought, *as it's your last.*

56

The pounding of the rain sunk to a distant murmur beneath the arch. Andy leant against the wall and slumped to the floor. Beams of light picked out the ornate details on the arch's grand ceiling. Andy peered up at it through unfocused eyes.

He rested his head against the stone. His teeth clattered with the cold. His feeble breaths billowed out in vast clouds. He lifted the bottle to his lips and poured what remained down his throat. He didn't want to feel the cold anymore. He was already freezing and expected the night to get colder still. He should try to go somewhere warm. He might not even survive the night in these thin wet clothes. But now he had no money.

The slabs beneath him suddenly felt comfortable. He sank further down the wall. His arms splayed across the ground. The groan of the city was just a rumour here. Andy's eyes became heavy, and the shuddering which wracked his chest subsided. Somehow, he now felt warmer. Warm and tired. His eyes closed. A voice in his head argued that it was bad to close his eyes. Going to sleep in this cold and hostile situation wasn't a good idea. But Andy couldn't help it. The concrete beneath him was warm. The tension from his shoulders relaxed. The pain and worry had gone. The night drifted away.

Andy's eyes shot open. The bright lights dazzled him. His body was heavy and numb. He lay on the concrete beneath the arch. He heard something. A voice nearby.

He blinked hard. He didn't know how much time had passed since he'd closed his eyes. It felt like seconds.

The voices came again. Nearer this time. A man and woman materialised from the night and walked beneath the arch. The man held an umbrella to protect them from the rain.

"Is it much further? You said the place was close." The woman's voice echoed around the enclosed space.

"Yes, just up here. It'll be worth the walk. It's such a great place," the man replied.

Andy blinked again.

The man guided the woman into the park's looming shadow with a hand on her waist.

A memory flashed through Andy's mind. It fired through sense and synapse and snapped his body like a shock. The memory came with a name — *Emma*.

With that memory, more arrived. Emma was his wife, and they had a son, Frankie. He remembered that too. Andy's eyes were wide open now. All impressions of tiredness gone.

The man led Emma into the park's unquiet gloom. Andy didn't know what Emma was doing out here with a man he didn't know. Andy struggled to his feet. His weak limbs shook. His chest ached. He coughed and held himself upright. He staggered forwards, using the wall for support. He peered out into the park.

"Emma," he whispered. How could he have forgotten about Emma?

Then he heard a sound which pounded through his ear drums.

57

A shrill scream echoed through the park. It resonated uselessly from the gaunt, rain-soaked trees, then faded to silence.

To Andy, holding the wall of the arch for support, the sound was as clear and sharp as a knife thrust. Andy knew he'd heard it. The place was empty.

Andy forced himself out into the night. He tried to shout, but his voice was just a rasp within his chest. Andy stumbled down a pitch-black pathway towards the noise. The occasional streetlight cast an island of light in the nebulous gloom.

"Hey! What's going on down there?" His voice was little more than a whisper.

Something moved in the shadows ahead. He lumbered on. His legs grew in strength with each dull thud against the slabs.

Another muted cry echoed through the park.

A man appeared from the night. He struggled with something. Andy squinted, paused, then saw the unmistakable glint of a blade.

Andy ran. He covered the distance in a few seconds. Each breath was a wound to his chest.

"Emma!" The words left his lips, but the sound was unheard.

His footsteps rumbled against the stones.

Andy slammed his full weight against the figure's back. The man groaned and stumbled forward. Andy clung on as the man's feet scrambled for grip. The man found his footing and turned. The knife glimmered menacingly.

The woman pulled herself away across the concrete and climbed to her feet.

Andy gritted his teeth and used all his strength to loop an elbow around the man's right hand. The hand which held the blade. He pulled the arm back. The man was powerful. The blade shook as both men strained to control it. The arm slid towards him. The glinting blade neared. Andy strained. The exertion burned his arms.

Something cold and hard sliced against his stomach.

Andy lashed out with his left hand but hit nothing but air. He tried again. His fist connected with something soft. He punched again. The man winced audibly. Andy felt what he thought was the man's wrist and grabbed it. He pulled the knife away from him again and struck out with an elbow.

The woman backed away from the scene. Her torn coat exposed her blue dress beneath. Her eyes were wild with fear.

The man broke free and pushed to his feet. Andy fell. Something clattered to the floor. Footsteps rumbled away.

"Emma," Andy whispered, raising a hand to his stomach. Blood ran between his fingers.

"I'm going to call for help," the woman said, rummaging through her handbag. Andy gazed up at her. The faraway light of a passing car flashed across her face before fading again.

Andy's breathing weakened now. The cold encompassed his entire body, and his need to sleep returned.

"Emma," he whispered again.

58

Leo's eyes shot open. The shrill of a ringing phone echoed through their room. His eyes scanned the ceiling.

"Answer it then," grumbled Allissa from the other bed in their twin room.

Leo rolled over and fumbled with the lamp.

Allissa swore.

Leo grabbed his phone from the bed-side table and answered without looking at the caller.

"Leo, it's Niki," came a frantic voice down the phone. She sounded as though she were on the move. Leo didn't have time to reply. "I've found your brother. He's in hospital. He's been stabbed."

59

He woke up tangled in the covers with a film of sweat covering his body. He forced himself out of bed. He'd fallen asleep with the heater on and the apartment was sweltering. He flicked it off and peered at the crack of morning light seeping through the dirty curtains.

Then, like a train out of control, the thoughts came back to him all at once. Some vagrant had prevented his masterpiece. That was not the way it was supposed to go. He should have laid him down too.

He examined the dingy apartment. He shouldn't be here either. This place was just for work, not for him to spend the night. Knowing the police would soon be on the streets, he'd panicked and fled. But he shouldn't have stayed here. He should have changed and then gone home.

He pulled aside the curtain and peered out.

The rain had worn itself out. The morning was bright and cold.

The rain had been good though, he thought. It washed

away any evidence which he may have left. In a torrent like that, fingerprints or DNA were scarce.

He wrapped his right hand around his left wrist. His fingers snaked up and down his damp skin. Nothing. His stomach tensed. He pulled the cover aside and stared at his wrist. The bracelet had gone. He tore the sheets from the bed. They came away bare. He yanked the bed away from the wall and searched behind it. He saw nothing but the grime of the apartment.

The bracelet was gone. It was the only thing his great-grandfather had kept after he'd lost the business. Engraved with his great-grandfather's name, they had passed it down through the generations.

He clenched his fists and thumped them against the wall.

He turned to the sepia-toned picture hanging above the bed. His great-grandfather sat upright, his head tilted backwards, looking away to the left of the camera. He held a domed hat between his hands and a row of military insignia — fakes, as his great-grandfather had never served in the military — glowed proudly from his chest.

"A great man," he whispered to the photograph. "And I will do you proud. You will see. You will see."

The police were going to be all over this now. That was a problem. They had one of his knives, and they probably had the bracelet.

That didn't matter.

The knife was clean, and unless they knew what they were searching for — which he very much doubted — the bracelet meant nothing.

He stripped and stuffed his clothes inside a black plastic bag. He would need to dispose of them as quickly as possible. He couldn't afford any more mistakes. He took a clean set of clothes from another bag and put them on.

He studied the room again. It was set up and waiting. A simple bed, simple furniture. The same things the great man had worked with. The same canvas on which to create the same masterpiece.

60

Leo couldn't pinpoint where or when his dislike for hospitals had begun. Although there wasn't a particular event that had put him off, every time he found himself in one, whether as a patient or a visitor, the walls closed in around him.

Maybe it was something to do with the constant light, the smell of the disinfectant or the subtle hum of machines. Maybe it was the hushed conversations, which he always assumed were about someone's life or death. Either way, as he watched Andy sleeping through the window from the waiting room, Leo felt the subtle throng of anxiety close around his chest.

He took a deep breath and tried to let it pass. He knew his anxiety now, and he could normally keep it under control.

Emma's shoes squeaked as she paced up and down the corridor behind him. Michael had dropped her off a few minutes after Leo and Allissa arrived. Allissa dozed in a plastic chair, her head leaning back against the wall.

"Breathe in, breathe out. Calm and focus." Leo repeated

the mantra to himself. The phrase had stopped him slipping into panic during several life-threatening situations.

It didn't seem to make any difference now. The constant hum of the building seeped into his skull. The thick, chemical taste clawed at his throat.

"I'm going to get some air," Leo said to Emma. "Come and fetch me if he wakes."

Emma stopped pacing, glanced at Leo and nodded. She was pale and gaunt — just an echo of her usual bright personality.

Avoiding the bank of elevators, Leo charged down three flights of stairs and into the reception. He waited to let a pair of nurses enter, their coats pulled tightly around blue uniforms. Leo couldn't understand how people worked in hospitals, although he had a boundless admiration for the fact they did.

He stepped out into the bruising morning and took a slow, long breath. The cold, fresh air slid deep into his lungs. He walked away from the entrance and slumped onto a bench. The rain which had sloshed through the city overnight had cleared and left the sky a harsh blue. It wasn't cold to Leo, though, it was revitalising.

He dug out his phone and counted the hours they'd been waiting for Andy to wake up. The doctor said that he should be awake by now. Why wasn't he? Was that a bad sign?

Andy had lost a lot of blood in the attack and was still very weak. The stab wound to the right side of his stomach was deep but could have been a lot worse.

Leo closed his eyes and focused on the wind beating at his face.

Andy had to make it. He had to.

But he could die. Leo's eyes flew open at the thought.

Andy could die, and leave Leo's sister without a husband and his nephew without a dad.

Sure, there were things Leo disliked about Andy. But he also knew Andy had it in him to be a good husband and father — he'd just lost his way. Andy could put that right if he had the chance. He needed to pull through this.

Leo rubbed his face and thought about the people he needed — his parents, his sister and Allissa.

Allissa. The woman who, in the last two years, without him even intending it, had become the focal point of his life.

A man and a woman ran together down the street. The woman strode out in front with her black hair swaying. Their colourful clothes shone in the early light.

"What're you thinking about?" The bench creaked as Allissa sat down beside Leo. "Silly question really, sorry."

Leo turned towards Allissa. The pink morning air softened her features. Her billowing breath mingled with his in the space between them.

"What was I thinking?" Leo asked.

Allissa wrapped her arms around herself and suppressed a shiver.

"I was thinking about you, actually," Leo said, staring deep into Allissa's eyes. The surrounding noise evaporated. Allissa smiled. She put her hand on top of Leo's on the bench.

Leo glanced down at their hands. Her touch warmed his skin. Leo pulled a deep breath of the morning air and leant towards Allissa.

"Your brother's awake."

Hearing the voice behind them, Leo and Allissa turned. Andy's nurse stood at the door. Leo and Allissa rose and followed her back inside.

"Be aware, he's confused at the moment," the nurse

warned them at the door of Andy's room. "You can only stay for a few minutes."

Leo nodded. Emma held Leo's arm tightly. The nurse opened the door.

"I can't," Emma said, freezing as she saw the instruments which monitored Andy's vital signs.

"He's going to be —" Leo said.

"No. You go first. Give me a minute."

Leo followed the nurse inside.

"What's happening?" came Andy's groggy voice as they entered the room.

61

Rosy morning light cut through the room as Andy struggled to open his eyes. He tried to glance around, but everything was too bright. He couldn't make sense of it. A calm voice spoke, but he couldn't make out the words. He closed his eyes again and tried to remember what he'd seen before unconsciousness overtook him. Night had fallen — long shadows hung like ghostly fingers, it was raining — drops of water hammered against his skin. Thunder rumbled angrily. He was cold. A shiver shook through him at the memory.

He didn't feel cold now, though. He was warm.

He hadn't been alone, Andy remembered that. There had been a woman.

"Emma?"

Andy wasn't sure if he'd spoken the words out loud.

"Emma!"

With the name came other memories. They pounded the surface of his mind like rain on the city streets. He remembered the knife flickering in the gloom. The sharp pain in his stomach. The woman's muted cries.

"Emma."

He forced his eyes open again. The light still dazzled, but he fought against it. He resisted the temptation to let them close. His eyes throbbed. The room struggled into focus. He was on a bed. Shapes moved around him.

The voice came again. It was reassuring. Then something touched his arm.

His vision twisted and strained further into focus.

"Emma?"

Andy gazed up. Faces surrounded him, but Emma wasn't there. One was a nurse. She glanced from him to a screen beside his bed and then adjusted something.

The other was a man. Andy studied him for long seconds as recognition dawned. A name floated into Andy's mind.

"Leo," he said, finally. "What's... what's going on? What are you doing here?"

Leo didn't reply.

"I don't know what's happened," Andy said. "I can't feel my —"

"That's just the painkillers," the nurse said, turning from readings. "You'll feel a bit out of it for a while."

Andy nodded.

"This needs to stop." Leo stepped forward and put his hands on the foot of the bed.

"What —"

"My sister, your wife, hasn't stopped crying in two days because of what you've done."

"Emma," Andy said, his expression melting. "Is she okay?"

"Not really," Leo said. "She'd be better off without you."

"She wasn't attacked?"

"No."

"We've been staying at my brother's apartment in Hoboken," Andy said, surprising himself with the memory. It was now making sense.

"You were, yes," Leo said, "before you stole money, and their car. The car which you crashed because you were so drunk."

Andy squirmed beneath Leo's unrelenting stare. It was a conversation Leo had wanted to have for a long time.

Andy stared at his feet.

"You could have died in that car," Leo said, "or killed someone else. Then you'd never have been able to see your son again."

"Frankie." Andy's eyes shot to Leo's.

"He's doing fine. Missing his dad, though."

Andy inhaled. Tears sparkled.

Leo watched him impassively.

Andy was no longer the man who terrorised Leo about his lifestyle decisions, treated his wife as a servant or disrespected the generosity of her parents.

"You guys have things to catch up on," the nurse said, sliding a clipboard onto the foot of the bed. "He's tired, so don't stay too long. Press the call button if you need anything."

The noise of the hospital streamed in as the nurse opened the door and disappeared out into the ward. A trolley clanged past and somewhere a TV played.

"I don't know," Andy said, finally.

"You don't know what?"

"I don't know what happened. I don't know what to do." Andy was becoming more upset now. "I don't know how to be Frankie's dad."

Leo watched the man crumple further into the bed.

"You're all new to it," Leo said, his voice softening. "You

just need to do what you think is right for him. You're allowed to make mistakes —"

"But I —"

"But first," Leo cut in, "you need to be there, and you need to be sober."

Andy stared at Leo. Leo thought he was going to argue, but he didn't. He stared back down at the bed without a word.

"I'm not sure Emma will even want me back now," Andy said.

"I don't know," Leo said. "It wouldn't be surprising if she didn't. She spends all her time with a child who doesn't really speak yet. Then you come home in a foul mood because you hate your job and just start drinking."

"But I... I need to work," he said, "we need the money."

"We both know Emma's offered to go back to work instead. She loved her job, and it paid better than yours. Then you could get to know your son."

"But that's not what a dad does," Andy said with failing conviction.

"If a dad is someone who drinks too much, then Frankie doesn't need one," Leo said. "He can just as well do without that."

Andy nodded morosely.

"I'm not telling you what's best," Leo said. "I am telling you to talk to your wife, discuss it and be open to it. Together you'll make a definition of being that boy's father that works for you all."

Leo let the comment sit for a minute.

"Did you get that from Michael too?" Leo said, pointing to a clear plastic bag on the bedside table which looked as though it contained a watch or bracelet.

Andy turned his head and winced.

"I don't know." Andy picked up the bag and tipped it out on the bed. "No, this isn't. I don't —"

Andy stopped speaking as the door whispered open, and he locked eyes with his wife.

62

"No, Mrs Everdeen," Niki said, her posture rigid. "I've tailed him ten times in the last two months. To and from work. To the golf club at the weekend. For drinks and jazz on Bleecker Street. I found nothing to prove your husband is having an affair."

The woman opposite Niki dabbed dramatically at her eyes with a silk handkerchief.

"I was just... well, I was just so sure," she said, her eyes roaming the room. "How can you know? Maybe he just got lucky. Could you continue for another month, or maybe two?"

Niki glanced at her hands on her lap. Of course, she didn't want to turn down work and Mrs Everdeen paid her well, but Niki knew there was nothing here. She had no reason to suspect her husband.

"Mrs Everdeen, this investigation is a waste of your money and my time. Your husband is not doing anything wrong. I suggest you seek the help of a marriage councillor as opposed to a private investigator."

Mrs Everdeen's eyes widened and then narrowed again.

"I don't... Well, I'm not..." Mrs Everdeen slid her handkerchief away, stood and stomped towards the door.

Niki leaned back into the chair and watched the large woman flounce from her office.

She swore and gazed at the ceiling. Was this really all the life of a private detective involved?

Niki stood and walked to the window. The street beyond was quiet and calm. It was midmorning, and the winter sun lit the city in gold and grey. The trees lining the street split her view into a skeletal patchwork of grey and brown.

Niki knew that what she needed to do was solve a case. A big case. A murder or disappearance, or something like that. That would be her opportunity to make a proper name for herself. Then she could drop working for all the jealous lovers and mistrusting marriages. A prominent case could change her professional life indefinitely.

Niki turned and rubbed her hands together. A case like the Downtown Ripper. Solving something like that was exactly what she needed. That would set her up for good.

Niki drew a newspaper from her bag and spread it across the coffee table. She flicked to page 4 for the full story on the Downtown Ripper. He'd tried to strike again last night, but he had been interrupted. Interrupted, coincidentally, by the guy those two British detectives were hunting.

Well, that's where I should start, Niki thought, straightening up. She'd done them a favour by finding their brother, or whoever it was. Now they could help her in return.

63

"That's another case solved then," Leo said as they stepped out into the midday light. They'd stayed in the hospital another hour as Emma and Andy had spoken. Then, when Michael and Nadia arrived with Frankie, Leo suggested they leave them to it.

The day was bright and cloudless. Although tired, he felt positive after the conversation with Andy.

"What did you say?" Allissa asked, doing up her coat and turning left.

"That's another case solved," Leo repeated, running a few paces to catch up with Allissa. "The missing person's been found. We can go home and chill."

The thought of home was a strange one. They'd been away for over three weeks. It had been such a busy time that Leo had barely thought of their small flat in Brighton. He was looking forward to being in a city he knew and taking his daily blustery run along the seafront.

"No, we can't go yet," Allissa said, turning left.

"Why? We came here to find Andy, and now we've found

him. Let's enjoy New York for a couple of days and then head back."

Allissa stopped and turned. Leo knew what was coming even before Allissa said it. He tried not to smile.

"Niki phoned while you were talking with Andy. She needs us to help her catch this serial killer."

"No way," Leo said, his palms extending outwards in mock surprise. "No way. We'll just pay her for the time. We're not the police here. That's their job."

"Andy's one of two people to see the killer and survive," Allissa said. "He can tell us everything he knows."

"We?" Leo said. "*We* have done everything we need to. *We* should leave now. Andy can talk to the police if he wants. What about the girl? The victim?"

"Niki says that the victim can't remember anything. She'd been drinking all night for a friend's birthday party. She's confused about the whole thing. We should return the favour to Niki."

"No," Leo said, fighting a smile. "Absolutely not. No way. It's not our thing."

"Okay," Allissa said. "We'll just go home and leave this madman killing people all over the city, because that's nothing to do with us, right?" Allissa folded her arms.

"Yes," Leo said, trying hard to keep a smile from breaking. "It's nothing to do with us. I've had about an hour's sleep and need to go to bed. Ask Niki how much we owe her, we'll get that paid, then enjoy a few days in New York. Then, we'll go home."

Allissa's stare intensified. "Sure, you go back to bed. I'll help Niki and see you when we've sorted this. Niki did us a massive good turn, and now she needs our help. Without her, we wouldn't even know that Andy was in the hospital until he remembered. I want to help her in return."

Leo held Allissa's glare.

"Besides, imagine how you'd feel if that woman last night was Emma, or me?"

As his smile broke like a sunrise, any anger in Leo's expression dissolved.

"What?" Allissa said through a scowl.

"Of course we're going to help Niki," Leo said, stepping towards her. "It just feels like a tradition for us to have this conversation now."

Allissa huffed, turned without a word, and started toward Niki's office in Greenwich Village.

64

He let the door of his apartment thump closed behind him. The place was so different from the decrepit apartment in Manhattan: expensively furnished, neat and clean. Although, the trimmings of wealth and fame brought him no pleasure now.

He crossed the room and sank onto the sofa. This place was like a mask to him. It exuded a personality he didn't think fitted him any longer.

He ran his hand across his trousers where he usually concealed the knife. That's what made him feel good now. That's what made him feel right. The merciless, exterminating steel of that blade. The tool of his trade.

It actually felt good staying in the other apartment. It felt right. There was something simple, honest and pure about the place. The place that he was about to make famous. Of course, he knew he shouldn't have stayed there. It was going to be the scene of a murder, and he needed to leave as little evidence as possible. The police would comb every detail from the crime scene. They would examine every fibre and mark.

But then again, did it really matter?

They could be damned incompetent. There were many cases where vital evidence was damaged or missed altogether.

He smiled. The police would be going mad trying to solve this. He imagined the detectives going wild over it. Pacing the floor, slamming fists against desks, shouting into phones.

Their problem was, he'd left them nothing to go on. His crimes had no pattern, no rhyme, and definitely no reason. The police had no clue where he was going next, and no indication of who he was. And then, before they caught up with him, he would drift back into his normal life. Right under their noses.

Of course, there was a backup plan too. Passports and money somewhere safe, just in case he needed to run. He could be out of the country in a matter of hours. South America maybe, or Europe. Who knows? London. He smiled. Turning up in London would be beautiful. The coincidence of it. The perfection of it. He could walk those streets just like —

He laid back into the sofa and gazed at the ceiling.

He was so close. So close to going down in history. And like last time, the police weren't even close.

He thought of the room. The scratchy bedsheets and the faint smell of damp. Spending time there before *she* was with him felt wrong. The place was incomplete without her, like a bird without its wings.

He clenched his left fist and remembered the blood dribbling through his fingers. Its warm embrace covered his skin. He felt that often now. He imagined that feeling every time he closed his eyes.

His heartbeat quickened as he longed to do it again. He couldn't wait to do it again.

He would do it again, and soon. And this time, no one would disturb him. She would be his. All his.

65

"But what do we know about this killer?" Allissa said as she skimmed the newspaper articles arranged on the coffee table in Niki's office. Colourful pictures of the young, beautiful women smiled up at her.

"He's opportunistic," Niki said. She laid out another printed article, then stood and folded her arms.

Allissa examined the four victims. Three had lost their lives, and one — thanks to Andy — had survived.

"He?" Allissa questioned.

"We assume it's a man, as most killers of this type are," Niki said.

"That makes sense, as he's targeting young and attractive women," Allissa said. "It pays to keep an open mind, though."

"Also, because the killings are so violent," Leo said from the side of the room where he was trying to operate the coffee machine. So far, all he'd been able to do was get it to emit an angry hiss of steam.

"Women can be violent too," Niki said.

"Of course," Leo agreed, "but the person who attacked

Andy was around the same size as him. He's, what, around six-foot —"

"six-one," Niki said, picking up a sheet of paper on which she'd already compiled a profile of the killer.

"Which suggests it's probably a man," Leo said, swearing as another cloud of steam thronged from the machine. He was struggling after his lack of sleep the previous night, and the coffee machine's reluctance to produce the goods was not helpful at all.

Niki paced the room.

"Has the surviving victim been able to say anything more yet?" Allissa asked.

"No, they hope she might in time. But not yet. She was drunk, apparently. Can hardly remember anything. She was out in town with friends, but they left her there. Just assumed she'd gone already."

"Nice people," Allissa said.

"Yeah," Niki agreed. "They can't remember who she was talking to either."

"How do you know all of this?" Allissa said.

"It was on the news this morning. Nothing stays out of the news in this city. Let's see if anything's changed." Niki tapped her smartphone, and a 24-hour news station appeared on the TV. A reporter was interviewing a man about last night's attempted murder.

"It's him again," Allissa said, pointing at the screen.

"Yeah," Niki agreed, "he's always on. I've no idea how he knows so much."

Another hiss of steam emanated from the coffee machine, followed by a barrage of swear words.

"I met him in the club last night," Allissa said. "While we were out searching for Andy."

"Really?" Niki asked, suddenly interested. "Did he say anything about the case?"

"He said he was swamped with all the interviews at the moment. I asked him about Andy because he'd been in the nightclub the night before too."

"What club was that?"

"Some place near Bleecker Street, Opus Jazz Club."

"That's where the victim was," Niki said, holding the notepad against her chest. "Although her friends didn't think she met the guy in there."

"You think the killer could have been there last night?" Allissa probed.

"It's possible,"

"Anyway, I gave this guy," — Allissa pointed at the man on the television — "my number in case he remembered anything about Andy." She dug out her phone. "He sent me a message this morning to ask if I wanted to go for a drink."

Niki's looked at Allissa. "What did you say?"

"Nothing yet —"

"I think I've finally got this nailed," Leo said, stepping over to the two women with three espressos on a tray. "Working that machine is like launching a..." He noticed Niki and Allissa's intense stares and trailed off. "What've I missed?"

66

Despite the modern trend for men of his age to let their stubble grow, he couldn't abide that. He loved shaving and did it the way his father had taught him. No electric razors or disposable blades here. He eyed himself in the mirror, foam coating his face. He picked up the shaving brush and finished applying foam to his cheeks.

He liked to imagine that men had been doing it this way for centuries. Before these times of instant gratification, you had to learn your craft. This was a craft.

He turned his face this way and that. Then applied a little more foam to his right cheek.

This was how his forefathers had prepared themselves. This was how his great-grandfather would have prepared himself — despite having a rather impressive moustache. He had considered the moustache in homage to the great man, but some things did move on with the times.

He washed his hands then dried them on a towel. When they were dry, he slung the towel across his shoulder. He lifted the blade with reverence from the side of the sink. The cold steel felt good. Powerful. He ran the tip of his thumb across the sharpened edge. The smallest sliver of skin peeled away.

Then, with the grace of a dancer, he lifted his head and positioned the blade. The unforgiving steel nestled against his skin. The tool that was destined to separate. Only he would decide whether it was hair from flesh, or flesh from flesh.

His phone vibrated on the shelf beside the sink. His eyes flickered towards it. He fought the temptation to look.

The glory of the moment dissolved. He scowled, put down the blade and picked up the phone. He read the message and a smile spread across his foam-coated cheeks.

67

"Absolutely not," Leo said, sliding the tray of coffee onto the table so he could express his disgust with hand gestures too. The suggestion made him feel physically sick.

"We don't know who this guy is." Leo counted the reasons it was a terrible idea on his fingers. "We don't know that he's not involved. It might be dangerous." He'd expected to get further than three. "And —"

"And what?" Niki cut in, challenging him with a lopsided grin.

"It might be dangerous," Leo repeated.

"Oh, come on. Look at him," Allissa said, pointing at the man on the television. "We met him last night at the club. You were there too. Did he seem dangerous?"

"Maybe." Leo shrugged.

"If cheesy grins could kill, then I say maybe too," Allissa said. "He knows all about the case. It could be just what Niki — what *we* need, to solve this."

"It's alright. They'll be no danger at all. We'll tail them

too," Niki said. "They won't be out of our sight even for a second. Allissa's just going to use that womanly charm of hers to see if this guy knows anything we don't."

"Doesn't that make you question how he knows so much?" Leo pushed. He picked up an espresso and downed it.

"That's his job. He probably has informants in the police or something," Allissa suggested.

"If we can get a step ahead," Niki said, her voice softening, "if we can just get something that puts us ahead, then we could solve this. Do you know how great that would be for us all? All of our reputations? Imagine the kudos you'll get when you can tell people you beat the NYPD to catching the Downtown Ripper."

Leo glanced from Niki to Allissa and back again. "I'm not happy about it," he said.

"Why?" Niki replied, her eyes locking onto Leo's.

Leo saw Niki's lopsided grin and blushed. He shrugged, not knowing how to answer the question.

"Honestly," Allissa said, "it'll be fine. I'm just going to talk to him and see if he knows anything. As Niki said, you guys will be close too. You don't need to worry."

Leo looked at Allissa. A sickening feeling rose. He stared down at the tray of coffees.

"If you're sure," Leo relented, picking up another espresso. "You need to stay close by, and if anything at all seems funny, then you're out of there."

"Of course," Allissa said, nodding. She picked up her phone and typed a message.

The reply came quickly.

"It's arranged," Allissa said, now smiling. "We're meeting at the Broadway-Lafayette Metro at seven."

"Great." Niki glanced at the large clock on the wall. It was the sort that was more suited to a railway station than an office. "That gives us just over two hours. What do you need?"

Leo gazed out the window. The light of the afternoon was fading into evening. The muscular skyline of downtown Manhattan glinted in the nebulous sky. Leo lowered his eyes from the green and red roofs of Greenwich Village to a man and woman making their way down the street. They both wore long coats and walked arm in arm. Leo watched them silently.

"Well?" Leo heard Niki's voice. He turned to find her and Allissa staring at him.

"Is that okay?" Niki said when Leo didn't answer.

"Sorry," Leo said. "I was a million miles away."

"We're going to go back to my apartment to get Allissa changed. I've got a dress that this guy won't be able to take his eyes off. Meet us at the Broadway-Lafayette Metro at six-thirty." Niki took her coat from the hook by the door and adjusted her headscarf in the mirror.

Leo nodded reluctantly.

"See you there," Allissa said as she opened the door. Leo's and Allissa's eyes met for a moment before she disappeared out into the hallway.

"And Leo," Niki said, her hand resting on the door handle. "Get some sleep for an hour. You're no good to anyone like this. Oh, and don't be late. We need to be out of sight by the time he arrives."

"Sure, yes, good idea," Leo said as Niki pulled the door closed behind her.

Leo dropped to the sofa. *Get some sleep for an hour.*

He knew that he and Allissa were investigators. They would stop at nothing to get to the truth. Allissa meeting this man was all a part of that. It was *just* part of getting to the truth.

Get some sleep.

Leo knew that when he closed his eyes, however, all he would see in his mind's eye was Allissa and a faceless man walking arm in arm down the streets of New York.

68

"We'll have some further questions for you when you're feeling better, Mr Harris." A detective from the New York Police Department stood at the foot of Andy's bed. "Your bravery saved the life of a young woman last night."

"I'm sure anyone would have done the same." Andy nodded solemnly and then stifled a yawn. The day had been long and exhausting.

"You have the department's contact details," the detective said, pointing to the card in Andy's hand. "Call us if you remember anything more. Every detail, no matter how big or small, could make a difference here."

"Yes, of course," Andy said, this time failing to snuff out the yawn. He slid down lower in the bed.

"Get some rest. We'll speak again."

The detective walked to the door, reached out for the handle, then turned back to Andy.

"One more thing," he said, tapping his lower lip with his pen. "You don't happen to know how your brother's" — the detective glanced down at his notepad — "Porsche Boxster came to be abandoned in the Lincoln Tunnel, do you?"

Andy stared silently at the detective and shook his head.

"No? That's a shame. You know, it's funny. They were doing some maintenance on the tunnel's CCTV. I guess we'll never know." The detective turned and disappeared through the door.

Andy sighed. His brain ached from the realisations of the day, and he felt sick with how close he'd come to losing everything. He thought of Emma standing in the doorway just a few hours ago. Things were going to have to change. He and Emma would talk about it and work out the right thing to do.

Despite the physical and mental pain, Andy had a strange feeling that things would get better. They would work out.

He picked up the TV remote and clicked it on. He needed the friendly chatter to drown out the dismal sounds of the hospital. The TV glowed, and a 24-hour news station appeared on the screen. Andy fumbled with the remote until the volume increased.

"The Downtown Ripper attempted to claim his fourth victim last night." The voice of a news anchor-man filled the room. "Whoever he is, he's quickly becoming one of New York's most prolific serial killers. Two days ago, crime expert Seth Stryker said this..."

The image of the news presenter faded to one of a younger man. He was being interviewed somewhere in the city. Andy held up the remote control to change the channel. This was the last thing he needed to see. His fingers were hovering over the button when he noticed something. His breath caught in his throat, and his eyes went wide.

69

Allissa had always considered herself a confident person. She'd travelled the world on her own, met dozens, maybe even hundreds of people, and faced all sorts of dangers without ever really being scared.

But now, waiting outside the Broadway-Lafayette Metro station just before seven, her nerves circled like hungry vultures. Maybe it was the dress Niki had picked for her to wear. Made by a prominent Muslim fashion designer, the dress was far glitzier than Allissa would usually wear. Although it covered her from neck to wrist, it clung uncomfortably close to her skin.

Then she thought of Leo's reluctance. He wasn't happy that she was doing this. And although he'd conceded eventually, the entire exchange had made Allissa feel uncomfortable.

But I'll be fine, Allissa thought, pulling a smile in case Seth was nearby.

Allissa scanned the people on the opposite side of the road. A bright electronic billboard above them flicked from one product to another. Niki was watching from somewhere over there too. And, Allissa's phone was broadcasting her location to both Leo and Niki — a feature that had saved Leo's life in Berlin a few weeks before.

They'd been through their plan on the short walk from Niki's apartment. Nothing was going to go wrong.

Still, there was something that worried her. Something in the look Leo had given her as she'd left Niki's office. It was a new one, and Allissa didn't know how to read it.

Allissa spotted Seth climbing the stairs of the metro station, pinned a smile to her face, and forced the worries from her mind. It was going to be alright. It would definitely be fine.

70

Night had fallen by the time Leo awoke. The large windows, which earlier had piled light into the office, now swirled with the unsettled night.

Leo swore and sat up in a panic.

His short sleep had been a torturous one. Visions of people walking hand in hand down New York's tree-lined avenues swirled through his mind. In the dreams, one of those people was Allissa, and the other was a faceless man who held her hand and made her smile and laugh.

Leo gazed up at the clock. It was just after seven.

"Shit!"

He was late. Allissa may already be with Seth.

Leo grabbed his jacket and phone and ran down the stairs. Six messages waited from Allissa and Niki explaining the plan. Leo thumbed their location into his phone and pushed through the door out into the street.

71

"Yeah, although traditional news, TV, radio and newspapers are great," Seth said as they turned left onto Bleecker Street, "they just don't have the speed or the responsiveness that I do. Let me give you an example." They waited for a taxi to crawl past before crossing the road. When they were on the opposite pavement, Seth continued. "Traditional news people have to produce a set amount of content. If they have half an hour, they need to fill half an hour. If they have a hundred pages, they need to fill a hundred pages. I'm not like that."

"No?" Allissa asked, glancing up at him. His unblemished skin and high cheekbones shone beneath a streetlight.

"No, I only write things that interest my readers. I don't just fill pages for the sake of it. All killer, no filler." Seth smiled at his joke.

Allissa thought of the sensationalised 'Ten Worst Serial Killers of All Time' article she'd read an hour before, but kept quiet.

"That makes sense, I suppose," she said. "What have you been working on this week?"

"Oh, it's been all about this Downtown Ripper. Have you heard of him?"

"I've seen a couple of headlines," Allissa lied, turning to glance at Seth. "There's not been another victim, has there?"

"Yes, didn't you know? Last night. Well, an attempted one. Some hero fought him off."

"Wow," Allissa replied.

"Let's go here," Seth said, pointing at an Italian restaurant on the left. "One of my favourite places."

72

One of the great misconceptions about following people — Niki knew from experience — was that you had to be behind them. In fact, although you were more noticeable in front, anyone who expected to be followed spent so long worrying about what was behind them, they always missed the lady in the colourful headscarf fifty-feet ahead. Today was no different.

Niki paused at the window of a long-closed café and glanced behind her. Seth was doing all the talking and couldn't take his eyes off Allissa. The long faux-fur coat and the dress Niki had chosen were working wonders.

Niki set off again before Allissa and Seth neared. After a hundred yards, she slowed her pace and glanced over her shoulder. She didn't want them getting too close.

She paused at the window of a cocktail bar and turned. The street behind her was empty. Niki felt a moment of panic. They couldn't have slipped into a backstreet without her noticing.

The door of a restaurant on the opposite side of the road

thumped closed. Niki glanced through the restaurant's large windows. Inside, a waiter showed Seth and Allissa to a table.

73

Leo didn't notice the sound of laughter and the smell of food drifting from bars and restaurants as he rushed towards Allissa. His mind throbbed with the image of Allissa and the man.

His phone said that the journey to the metro station would take seventeen minutes. It seemed to last forever. Perspiration prickled his neck. He needed to be there, just in case something happened.

How could he have fallen asleep? All he had to do was be there on time, and now, now —

He couldn't even consider what might happen if he wasn't there on time.

Leo didn't notice the figure step from a shaded doorway. His mind was too busy tumbling with worst-case scenarios to see anything. His trainers sloshed through a puddle. He didn't notice the figure reach out behind him. He only noticed when the figure's arm closed around him and pulled him to a stop.

"Stop, come here," Niki hissed, pulling Leo behind a

tree. "Keep running up there, and they'll see you. They're in that restaurant." She pointed at an Italian restaurant across the street. "Where were you?"

"I was... I was —" Leo bent over, panting.

"Don't worry now," Niki said, releasing her grip on Leo's arm but not before pulling him up.

They peered through the restaurant's window.

"We'll go in that bar opposite," Niki said. "I'll go first and check there's a table where we'll have eyes on. I'll send you a message in two minutes."

Leo nodded breathlessly and dug out his phone. Niki disappeared inside the bar. Leo watched Allissa and Seth settle into their seats. A waiter in a red jacket gave them each a large menu. Seth talked, and Allissa glanced from him to the menu and back again.

Leo's phone vibrated in his hand. Niki had found them a table. He tore his eyes from Allissa, hurried down the street and pushed through the door of the bar. Sure enough, Niki sat at a table by the window.

"She looks great, doesn't she," Niki said as Leo slid into the seat opposite.

The restaurant was only thirty-feet away.

"Yeah, she does." Leo studied the shimmering fabric that clung to Allissa's body.

Niki turned to Leo and opened her mouth as though about to start speaking. Then she thought better of it and stopped. She glanced at the bar.

"Orange juice please," she said, pulling a small pair of binoculars from her bag.

"Right, yeah, sure." Leo climbed to his feet and headed to the bar.

Drinkers occupied most of the surrounding tables. It

was lucky they'd got the one in the window. Leo ordered an orange juice for Niki and a strong coffee for himself. He had the feeling it was going to be a long night.

74

Andy watched, his jaw slack and his eyes wide. The young man on the television postulated inanely about the Downtown Ripper. It wasn't the content of the conversation that shocked him, though. It wasn't the man himself. It was what gleamed from the man's left wrist.

Andy hit the pause button. The TV image juddered to the stop. The sleeve of the man's shirt was rolled up, and on his left wrist, in the New York winter sun of two days ago, hung a gold bracelet.

Andy grabbed the plastic bag from the bedside table and tore it open. The gold bracelet fell to the bedcovers. Andy picked it up and held it in front of the screen. It could be the same one, but from this distance, he couldn't be sure. The television was at least ten-feet away on the far wall. Andy pulled out the bedsheet, swung his legs over the edge and planted his feet on the floor. He rubbed his thighs to get some blood flowing around his numb legs. Slowly, he pushed himself upwards. His legs shook, but sustained the weight. Stabbing pains shot through his abdomen. Andy winced and almost collapsed backwards. He held firm, and the pain subsided.

With incredible effort, Andy reached the foot of the bed. The television was now just three-feet away. The paused image flickered on the screen. Andy held onto the foot of the bed with one hand and raised the bracelet with the other. He dangled it next to the image on the screen.

The bracelet he held had a gold chain attached to a small gold plate. He examined the plate carefully and spun it in his hands. They were the same. The same bracelets. Andy was sure of it.

Andy glanced back at the man on the screen. *Seth Stryker — True Crime Blogger,* the overlaid banner said.

Then he examined the bracelet and tried to make out the engraving. Andy couldn't quite see it in the low light. He reached across to the light switch beside the bed. His hand slipped. Andy leant sideways. He tried to catch his balance. His arms flailed. His leg slid across the floor. His side ached. Something tore from his arm, and an alarm sounded. Andy crashed to the floor.

75

Seth was still talking about his website when the food arrived. Allissa had hoped they'd just go for a pint somewhere, but to get the most out of Seth, she figured she should let him choose the place. Allissa glanced through the window as the waiter slid her penne arrabbiata onto the table. The restaurant's neon lights bathed the street in red. She knew Leo and Niki were nearby, but she couldn't see them from here.

"You know why I like this restaurant?" Seth said, picking up his knife and cutting into the sirloin steak. "They know how to do a rare steak. So often you ask for rare, and it comes medium. I mean, it's not that difficult. A couple of minutes on either side. But this," — he pointed at the meat from which blood oozed — "is perfect. Just perfect." He put it in his mouth and chewed.

Allissa picked up her fork and dug it into the pasta.

"What makes a great story for you? What do your readers really go for?" Allissa asked, taking a mouthful of the pasta. It was good.

Allissa now wanted to get on to what Seth knew about the Downtown Ripper.

"They like the gritty stuff. The killer who did all kinds of bad stuff and got away with it." Seth cut and ate another mouthful of steak. "I'm not sure why, but there seems to be something about those killers who've outsmarted the police. People seem to be interested in them."

"Do you think this Downtown Ripper will be like that?"

Seth's eyebrows bunched as he chewed. He coughed, then took a sip of water.

"Well, I don't know for sure," he said. "He's certainly captured the public interest."

"He?" Allissa said, nonchalantly.

Seth's eyes froze on Allissa.

"Well, it's bound to be a man. Female serial killers are rare, and this has all the hallmarks of a man."

"Such as?" Allissa prompted.

"His choice of targets, for example. Women. Each of a similar age —"

"So, you think his motivations are sexual?" Allissa chewed the pasta.

Seth stopped eating. The steak lay abandoned. A trickle of blood pooled across his plate.

"No. Well, I'm not sure, but as far as I know"— Seth picked up a blood-stained chip — "he hasn't raped them or anything. It's just a matter of killing them."

"What sort of person are we looking for then?"

Seth sat up a little straighter. He didn't answer at first.

"I'm just interested," Allissa said, twisting her fork in the dish, "as it's not often you get an audience with a murder expert." She smiled, and Seth's face twisted into a grin.

"Well, let's see. What do we know? He's quite a confident person."

"Why do you think that?"

"There doesn't seem to be any link between him and the victims. Well, I mean, any link that the police know yet, anyway. That means he's probably meeting them on the night, right before killing them."

Allissa nodded. "You think he just passes them in the street?" Allissa said.

Seth cut into the meat again. "Yes, something like that, I imagine." He gesticulated with his steak knife. The serrated blade was stained in blood.

"He must be quite a young guy then," Allissa suggested.

"What makes you think that?"

"If girls of that age are going to go with him willingly. There's no sign that he's forced them. None of them had any known history of prostitution. That makes me think he's a similar age."

"You're good at this," Seth said, nodding. "What do you say I get the check here and we head on somewhere a little more relaxing?"

Allissa glanced from Seth down to the bleeding hunk of meat on his plate.

"Sure," Allissa said.

76

Leo watched Allissa and Seth chatting in the restaurant across the road. He wasn't sure what he'd hoped for, but it certainly wasn't for Allissa to enjoy herself. There should at least be some long silences, awkward glances and inappropriate comments.

Leo sipped his coffee. The caffeine was helping. He watched Allissa lift a forkful of pasta to her mouth and chew.

Leo thought they were just going for drinks, not a meal.

"Mic check, one, two, three." The universal noise of a band checking the sound system echoed through the bar. The band's four members stood on a small stage at the back of the venue. A guy fussed around them, arranging microphones and plugging things in. The noise was the last thing Leo needed.

"How long have you guys known each other?" Niki asked Leo.

"About two years."

"How'd you meet?"

A bass guitar twanged from the stage. Leo raised his

voice and briefly explained the events that had brought them together in Kathmandu. Niki listened with interest.

"You know, you could just tell her," Niki said, cutting through the sound.

The drummer hit the snare drum as an engineer tweaked the sound.

"Sorry?" Leo said, turning to face Niki.

"Well, it's none of my business, but if there's something you want to talk to her about," — she pointed at Allissa who, was now dominating the conversation — "then you should do it. Life's way too short to mess about with things like that."

Leo flushed in the bar's gloom. Niki's intense stare bored into him. Leo stared back towards Allissa, but that seemed awkward too, so he stared at his hands.

"You obviously like each other though, right?" Niki asked, and her lopsided smile invited Leo's honestly.

"Yeah, of course. She's amazing."

"Do you think there's more to it than that?"

"I don't know," Leo said, "as we've never really talked about it."

The lead guitar took over. Sound warbled through the venue as the guitarist's fingers slid across the strings.

Leo's eyes met Niki's.

"I've spent the last fifteen years working with relationships that have broken down," Niki said. "Cheating partners, hidden mistresses. Heck, I've even seen a whole hidden family once or twice."

Leo smiled.

"What I mean is, I think I know when there's something between two people."

"Yeah," Leo said, turning to face Allissa across the street. Allissa pointed her fork at Seth as she asked a question. She brought so much to his life, and he loved the time they spent together. Something inside his chest fluttered, and he smiled unexpectedly.

"Yeah, she's incredible, isn't she?" Leo said at the same time as the music cut out. His loud voice carried across the silent room. Leo blushed. Niki laughed out loud.

"She sure is," — Niki touched Leo's arm — "and you should tell her so."

Without the noise from the band, Leo heard his phone ringing. He fumbled it from his pocket.

"It's Andy," Leo said.

"Go out the back and answer it," Niki said, pointing to a door beside the stage.

"Hold on," Leo said into the phone, "I'll just go outside."

Music thronged from the stage as the band broke into their first song. Leo shoved through the back door and out into a quiet side street.

"Hey," Leo said, "how're you feeling?"

"Leo, Leo," Andy said urgently. An alarm shrieked down the line, and there were other voices in the background too. "I know who the Downtown Ripper is."

The blood drained from Leo's face as he listened to Andy's explanation. The world stood still. The rumbling music from inside the bar faded to a whisper, and the air thinned to nothing. He extended his arm, leant on the wall and inhaled two long breaths.

"Leo, did you hear that? Does that make sense?" Andy said.

"Allissa."

"What?" Andy yelled. The alarm had stopped, but voices continued to chatter in the background.

Leo inhaled another deep breath. The world moved again. The volume of the band increased.

"Allissa's with Seth Stryker now," Leo said, his voice a shriek against the wall of sound. "I've got to go. Andy, thank you, I'll —"

The back door of the bar crashed open, and Niki flew out into the yard.

"Leo," she said as she grabbed him by the arm. "They've gone!"

77

Seth grinned as he directed Allissa towards the restaurant's rear door. He'd explained that it would be easier to get a taxi from the busier road at the back of the restaurant.

Allissa's dress shimmered as she walked ahead of him. Seth liked it. It looked good. They approached the door, and a waiter held out their coats. Seth slipped into his and then stepped forward to help Allissa with hers.

"Allow me," Seth said, taking her handbag.

Allissa thanked him and slipped into the large, faux-fur-lined coat. Seth stared down at the handbag. It contained a purse, a mobile phone and a few items of make-up.

Last night in the club, Allissa had been with a man. Although he wasn't here now, Seth didn't want him calling later.

He glanced at Allissa struggling with the buttons on the coat. He fished out her phone and slid it into his pocket.

"Thanks," Allissa said as she accepted the bag and tucked it beneath her arm.

The waiter held open the door. Seth and Allissa stepped out into the rain.

"Which way?" Allissa asked.

Seth glanced around for a taxi. It was darker at this side of the restaurant. He liked that.

A taxi turned the corner and headed their way. Its green 'For Hire' light skipped across the tarmac.

"We need to get a taxi," he said, pointing towards the glowing light.

Allissa's eyes darted towards the approaching vehicle. Seth noticed a flicker in her eyes. He wasn't sure what it was. Perhaps fear? He liked that too.

"It's not far away," Seth said, raising his hand towards the approaching taxi. The vehicle indicated and pulled to the kerb. "But it's a horrible night. We want to get there dry."

"Sure," Allissa said, clutching her bag. "It is cold. Where is this place?"

Seth opened the rear door of the taxi. "After you."

As Allissa slid into the car, Seth turned, pulled Allissa's phone from his pocket and threw it behind one of the ornamental olive trees beside the restaurant's door.

"It's not far at all," he said, getting into the taxi and slamming the door. "A few minutes. I'm looking forward to showing you one of my favourite places."

This was going to be easier than he thought.

78

"What do you mean they've gone?" Leo asked.

"I was watching the restaurant," Niki said, raising her voice above the band's rumbling bass. "Seth got up, I assumed he was going to the toilet, then Allissa got up, and no one came back. They must have gone out another way as they didn't come out the front."

Leo charged back through the bar, pushed past the crowd and gazed out at the restaurant. The table where Allissa and Seth had been eating was empty.

"It'll be okay," Niki said, her voice raised against the band. "Allissa's doing a great job. They've probably just moved on to have a cocktail."

Leo shook his head.

"What?" Niki asked.

"It's him," Leo said, leading Niki out onto the street. "Seth's the Downtown Ripper."

Leo explained to Niki what Andy had said on the phone. Niki's expression dropped. Her mouth moved, but no words came out.

Niki turned and crossed the road, then stormed through the restaurant's front door. Leo followed.

The restaurant was quiet. A piano tinkled somewhere, and the sound of dinnertime conversation bubbled.

"I need to know where the people who were eating at that table went," Niki demanded, marching up to the nearest waiter.

"I'm just serving these gentlemen —"

Niki pulled the notepad from the waiter's hands. "I need to know about those people right now!" Niki said. "It's urgent."

A hush settled over the restaurant as diners turned to face Niki and Leo.

"They left about two minutes ago," said a man from the table next to where Allissa and Seth had been. "I saw them. They used the other door, that way." He pointed to the back of the restaurant.

Niki put the waiter's notepad down and rushed through the restaurant.

"Thank you," Leo said, turning after her.

"Two people left this way?" Niki shouted at a waiter standing near the restaurant's rear door. The restaurant was deceptively big inside. Waiters moved sedately between candle-lit tables.

"Sure," the waiter said, offering a brief description. "Just a couple of minutes ago. They wanted a taxi. You might just catch them."

Leo and Niki barged out into the rain. The lights of a taxi, long streaks of red on the wet tarmac, turned right at the end of the street.

"Shit," Leo said as he watched it go. It was too far to chase. "It's alright though. We've got this system which tracks each other's phones in case we get separated." Leo loaded the map. Allissa's phone was just three feet away. He dialled her number. Her phone glowed from the pavement behind an ornamental olive tree.

79

"Now don't you try getting up again," the nurse said to Andy, tucking him tightly back into the bed. "You've had a very serious injury, and any movement could open the wound up again. You need to rest. Am I clear?"

Andy knew that although the nurse's voice was kind, he was getting royally told off. He nodded and stared down at his hands above the bedsheets.

"Is there anything you need before I go?" she asked.

"Yes, my phone, please." Andy turned, and with some effort pointed at the phone on the bedside table. Emma had dropped it in earlier. Fortunately, he'd left it in the apartment before leaving on his rampage three days ago. "Thank you," he said.

The nurse turned and left the room.

Andy watched the door click back into place and then opened his hand. The gold bracelet gleamed in his palm. While he'd been on the floor, alarms screaming and feet pounding towards him, he'd noticed a name engraved on it. *William Stryker.*

Andy unlocked his phone and typed the name into an internet search. Several articles appeared. Suddenly things made horrible sense.

80

Leo's heart thundered in his chest. He needed to think. His chest tightened. His breathing became frantic. Anxiety threatened to suffocate him. He leaned against the wall and fought for control.

Allissa was a feisty, fiery young woman who, alongside Leo, had faced down the barrel of a gun. This was different. Leo knew, almost beyond a doubt, that Seth was a serial killer. A serial killer who was now in a taxi with Allissa. A serial killer who intended for her to be his next victim.

Leo thought of them swimming together just days ago in St Lucia. He banished the thought. He needed to focus. He needed to work out what to do next.

"Your phone," Niki said, snapping Leo from his thoughts.

"What?"

"Your phone's ringing."

Leo glanced down. Andy was calling again. Leo swiped the screen, and Andy's voice came through.

"Hold on," Leo said, ducking along with Niki into the

restaurant's doorway. "Say that again. I'm putting you on speaker so Niki can hear too."

"There's an inscription on the chain!" Andy shouted excitedly. "William Stryker. I've just checked his name, and listen to this." Andy read from the page. "William Stryker 1832-1896, a New York based doctor and entrepreneur who became infamous after being accused of the Jack the Ripper killings in London in 1889. Stryker had built a large medical business and was in London in the autumn when the killings occurred. Before they could arrest him, he fled back to New York. Scotland Yard could not find enough evidence to extradite him to London, but with the publicity surrounding the allegations, Stryker's business collapsed. He died in poverty five years later."

"Probably his great-great-grandfather, or something like that." Leo's mind was running in overdrive now. "No wonder he has such an interest in historical crimes. But what are the similarities between the killings?"

Niki grabbed her phone and typed furiously.

"There were five known Ripper victims," Niki read. "Mary Ann Nichols, Anne Chapman —"

"Wait, wait," Leo said, "where were the bodies found?"

Niki tapped away again.

"They discovered Mary Ann Nichols on Friday thirty-first of August in Buck's Row. A week later, Annie Chapman on Hanbury Street. Elizabeth Stride in Dutfield's yard — shit." Niki prodded at the screen, unable to verbalise her realisation.

"Seth killed his first victim beside Dr Buck's cosmetic surgery," Leo said. "The second outside Hanbury's clothes shop, the third beside Dutfield's Diner."

"Then there was Mitre Square," Niki said, "and Andy stopped the murder in Washington Square."

"Where now?"

"Thirteen Miller's Court." Andy's voice startled Leo. "Mary Jane Kelly was murdered at Thirteen Miller's Court."

"You'll never guess what," Niki said, looking up at Leo. "There's an apartment building called Miller's Court. It's two miles away."

81

"It's a great city, isn't it?" Seth said, glancing at Allissa beside him in the back of the taxi. Allissa watched the buildings stream past. The weather had turned, and angry fingers of rain slashed at the glass.

"Yeah, I've not been before." Allissa turned to face Seth. His face glowed red from the taillights of the car in front.

"How long are you staying?"

"Just a couple more days, I think. We do a lot of travelling but often miss the best bits."

"I know exactly what you mean," Seth said, leaning towards her. "Who are you here with? Oh yes, your business partner. What's his name?"

"Leo," Allissa told him, suddenly hoping Leo and Niki were following them alright.

"Yes, that's it," Seth said. "Doesn't he mind you meeting up with other men like this?"

"No, we're," — Allissa thought about the best way to explain — "it's not like that. We're business partners. Is this place much further? I'm going to have to be going soon."

"Not far at all." Seth peered through the windscreen. It

was raining harder now. The outside world melted into crimson slashes of water against the window.

"Okay," Allissa said, gripping her bag against her lap. One more drink and then she was getting out of here. Seth was getting weirder by the minute.

82

Andy sat up in the hospital bed. Allissa was in danger. Although he didn't know Allissa — he'd been drunk the one time they'd met — she was close to Leo. Leo, Andy now realised, was family. That made Allissa important to him, too. He couldn't let anything happen to Allissa. Before Leo disconnected the call, Andy heard him say that Miller's Court was two miles away. That shouldn't take Leo and Niki more than a few minutes in light traffic. But what if that wasn't quick enough? What if Leo and Niki got there, and it was already too late? Andy couldn't acknowledge the thought.

He brought up the map of New York on his phone. The map zoomed in to show him Miller's Court. He zoomed out to see where Leo and Niki were coming from. He saw a pulsing blue dot just a few hundred meters from Miller's Court. That was his location. He was close. Andy tapped the screen and calculated the distance. He could be there, if he walked fast enough, in just a couple of minutes. He had to do something. He couldn't just stay here.

He rolled over and peered through the door's glass

panel. The corridor outside was quiet. The chatter of daytime visitors had finished hours ago. Andy pulled off the covers, turned his body, and slowly planted his feet on the floor. Each movement sent ripples of pain through his side. He lifted the hospital gown and examined the large bandage on his stomach. Winching, he peeled it away and glanced inside. Stitches pulled a three-inch gash into an angry smirk. This was going to hurt.

Fortunately, they'd taken him off that bleeping machine.

Andy bent down — teeth clenching with the pain — and picked up the bag of clothes Michael had given him. The kindness made Andy quite emotional. He'd stolen from his brother, yet Michael brought him clothes.

Andy dressed as quickly as possible then pushed his feet into the shoes. Bending to do them up caused shock waves of pain through his stomach. He took the shoes off, tucked the laces inside, then slipped them on.

Using the bed for support, Andy stood up and took a deep breath. The room wobbled around him. He straightened up, and slowly, carefully, crossed to the door.

He pushed the door open an inch or two and peered out into the corridor. The nurses' station opposite was empty.

Andy turned off the light, slipped out into the corridor and walked — painfully — towards the lifts.

83

"Two miles, two miles," Leo said, pacing up and down outside the restaurant. His panic had subsided now, and adrenaline thumped through his body.

Not a single car had passed. Niki glanced left and right for the welcoming lights of a taxi. She eyed her phone. The taxi app said the nearest car was six minutes away. The three minutes they'd waited already felt like hours.

"It shouldn't be long. There're always taxis around here," Niki said for the sixth time.

The throaty drone of a motor echoed between the buildings somewhere. Tyres swished across the wet road as a car passed out of sight.

Leo pushed his sodden hair from his face. It was raining again now, but he hardly noticed.

"I can run two miles in less than ten minutes," Leo said. He programmed the location on his phone. It wasn't far. He was used to running more than that every day. "I can do that in ten minutes. It could take that long just to get a taxi. I'll see you there."

Leo set off before Niki could reply. His feet pounded through puddles. Leo knew he could do this. He'd run as exercise and to clear his mind for years. He could make the two mile journey quicker than a taxi. It was a straightforward journey too.

He reached the first corner, glanced at the directions on his phone and barrelled to the left. A young couple leapt out of the way just in time to avoid a collision. Leo wished the distance away with each judder of his thumping feet. His knees ached with the vibrations. The thin soles of his shoes were not designed for running. Leo pushed the pain away.

He surged harder with each throbbing step. The sweat came. His arms pumped. Images of Allissa and Seth bombarded his mind. A car pulled out of a side street ahead. Leo charged in front of it. There was no time to stop. The driver protested on the horn. The sound faded into the restless noise of the city.

Leo pushed harder still as his legs normalised to the movement. His breathing dropped into sync. Acid burned his muscles. Time ticked. Distance dropped.

84

"Shit," Niki whispered, watching Leo charge ahead. There was no way she could keep up with him. She turned the other way. The street was dark and motionless. In a city of thirteen-thousand taxis, she was on the only street without one.

Niki glanced at her phone. Almost five minutes had elapsed since they'd charged into the restaurant on the tail of Allissa and Seth. Time was running out. Niki hunched her shoulders and exhaled. She spun again. Adrenaline rattled through her. She'd never had problems like this when she was tailing cheating partners through the backstreets.

An engine growled, and a horn ricocheted through the sheets of rain.

The door of the restaurant whispered open, and a couple peered out. Sounds of the restaurant rattled incongruously into the street. A tinkling piano played a cheerful jazz tune, and diners chattered.

"Hey Maurice, where's our taxi? We had it booked for five minutes ago," the woman at the door said.

"It'll be with you shortly mam," the waiter replied.

The orange halo of a taxi's lights slid around the corner. They shone from the dulled windows of a dozen shops.

"I need that taxi, sorry." Niki charged for the taxi, her arms raised above her head. She stomped through a puddle to block the taxi's progress.

The taxi squealed to a stop, and the driver pulled down his window. "I'm booked," he said.

"It's an emergency," Niki yelled. "I need to get to Miller's Court quickly."

"Not with me, miss. I'm booked." The driver edged the car forwards.

Niki stood in front of the taxi to prevent it from moving.

"You know the rules, miss. I'm booked!" the driver yelled.

"Fifty dollars for a ten-minute journey," Niki said, pulling out a note.

"Can't do it, now get out of the way." The driver edged the car further forwards.

"One-hundred then," Niki shouted.

The driver paused and registered Niki's determined expression. "Sure, okay." He nodded and unlocked the doors.

"Quick as you can." Niki slid into the back seat.

The woman who'd booked the taxi scowled from the restaurant's door.

"What's the hurry?" the driver said as he examined Niki in the rear-view mirror.

"If I told you, you wouldn't believe me." Niki dug out another fifty. "I'll give you another fifty bucks if you step on it."

"Yes ma'am." The driver accepted the notes and punched the accelerator.

New York

Niki stared from the taxi as the streets of New York flashed past.

She thought of Leo running there. They'd stop and pick him up if they passed.

Then Niki thought of the unspoken words hanging between Leo and Allissa. She'd sensed it from the first time they'd met. Tension like that could mean only one thing. When they got through this, she would make sure — personally — that conversation happened. She already knew exactly what to do. Life was way too short to mess about with things like that.

Niki grabbed her phone and dialled the emergency number. They would make it through this. They had to.

"Yes, NYPD."

Niki wasn't sure the police would take it seriously. It all sounded so far-fetched. She had to try.

The call connected and Niki explained everything to the operator.

A row of shuttered shops flashed past. People queued outside a nightclub. Warm lights glowed from apartment buildings and offices. All around the city, life was going on as usual. Yet in apartment thirteen at Miller's Court, something awful was about to happen.

"Come on, come on," Niki said, finally hanging up the phone. Not getting there in time was not an option.

85

"So where is this place?" Allissa said, following Seth out of the taxi. She probably knew everything about the case now, but didn't want to raise suspicions. She would go for one more drink and then call it a night. "It must be a really well-kept secret, down a street like this."

"Yes, it is." Seth led them away from the lights of the main road. The taxi clunked into gear and swished off into the rain. "It's one of those places very few people in New York know about. A real historical place."

"Right," Allissa said. She couldn't see anything down the gloomy road. She and Leo had visited many dingy backstreet pubs they wouldn't have known were there before, though.

A light above a shop flickered on and then died again. A downpipe sang with rainwater. A jet of ghostly steam wafted through a grate in the middle of the street. Somewhere far away, the shriek of a siren echoed like a mating call through the concrete jungle.

"Just up here," Seth said, dropping behind Allissa on the narrow pavement.

New York

Allissa squinted through the rain. A large concrete residential building reared upwards. Lights shone through the rain-streaked windows and residents hid behind filthy curtains. Beyond that, the road ended with a brick wall. Something scurried beneath a pile of rubbish. Lightning crackled through the heavens.

Allissa stared up at the building. Its six-story concrete outline loomed tall against the sky. The name — Miller's Court — crowned the entrance in discoloured letters. Lights from the door entry system winked.

The sirens were getting closer now. Allissa wondered where they were going.

"We must have gone the wrong way," Allissa said, turning to face Seth. He'd dropped a few paces behind her.

Seth moved his right hand behind his back as Allissa turned. His eyes burned like coals. Allissa suddenly felt very alone. Her hand instinctively moved towards her bag. Niki and Leo would be nearby. They must be. They were following her phone.

"I think... I'm going to call it a night," Allissa said, looking back at the main road beyond Seth.

A window opened in the building above them and the sounds of a TV show echoed out. An inane television audience laughed.

Allissa pictured herself and Leo back in their Chinatown hotel room, watching something mindless on the television. That's where they'd be soon.

"Oh, I'm not sure you should do that." Seth's voice was calm and deep. He didn't sound like the same man. "I think you'll come with me."

Allissa's hand slid inside her bag. It was time to call Niki and Leo and get out of here. Her fingers explored the contents of the bag. Allissa felt the shape of her purse, a tube of lipstick, but no phone. Her phone wasn't there. Allissa glanced down at her bag.

"I think you'll find you left your phone back at the restaurant," Seth hissed. He stepped closer, his hand still raised behind his back. His face twisted into a grin.

Allissa narrowed her eyes. This guy was taking the piss now.

"Right, well, I'd better go and get it." Allissa stepped around Seth and walked towards the main road. She'd spent enough time with this weirdo.

The main road was just a hundred feet up ahead. She'd get a taxi back to the restaurant, get her phone, then go back to their hotel.

A powerful arm closed around Allissa's neck and pulled her backwards.

"What the —" Allissa tried to shout.

She fell. Her feet slipped on the wet road. She hit something hard. The world around her juddered. The air left her lungs and rain fell directly into her face. She tried to scream. Only a whisper hissed into the night.

The ground shifted beneath her feet. She pushed against the arm and fought for breath. Allissa regained some composure. She pulled forward and drew a deep breath.

"What are you doing?" she snarled. Her hands balled into fists. "Let go of me now."

Allissa swung her right fist over her shoulder. It hit nothing but air. She tried again with her left elbow. It struck something. She went for it again. The elbow crunched, and Seth grunted.

"Let go of me now," Allissa shouted this time. "Let go of me or I'll kick the shit out of you, you fucking freak."

Seth's breath was heavy and warm on her neck.

Allissa changed tactic and stopped pulling away. She pushed back into Seth instead. He fell off balance and stumbled backwards. His grip around Allissa's neck stayed strong. They struck a wall. Seth groaned. Allissa felt the impact through his ribcage. Allissa crashed her right elbow twice into his face.

Then she stopped dead. It was sharp, clean and cold — the feeling of a knife against her throat. The pressure was light, but Seth held the blade firm. It wasn't pushing down on her skin, but slicing through it.

Allissa stopped struggling.

"You know what's going to happen now," Seth said. "It's all you've wanted to talk about all night."

Allissa searched the street with wild eyes. She searched for any movement. A passing vehicle or person. The window above them closed and the noise of the TV muted.

"It's you," Allissa said. "You're —"

"Surprise." Seth nuzzled his lips against her cheek. He inhaled and grunted with pleasure. "I've been looking forward to this. We're going to go down in history together."

86

"Miller's court, just down there on the right." The taxi driver skidded to a stop and pointed down a side street. A large concrete building jutted up into the night.

Niki leapt out of the taxi. The sombre shriek of sirens was close now. The police must have taken her seriously.

"Allissa!" Niki shouted. "Leo, are you here?"

She hadn't seen Leo on the drive across the city.

The street was quiet. Deserted. Niki ran into the looming shadow of Miller's Court. Most of the building's windows were dull against the orange city sky.

Something moved beside the door. A shuffle of feet. A muted voice. A dull thump.

"Allissa!" Niki shouted again.

Niki rummaged through her bag, pulled out a small torch and snapped it on. What she saw made her expression drop in fear. The bottom fell from her stomach.

Allissa stood beside the door. She was rigid and pale. Behind her, with a knife held against her slender neck, stood Seth.

Seth smiled. His teeth glistened in the torchlight. The whine of sirens rang again.

"Seth, it's over," Niki said. "You can hear the police. They'll be here any moment."

"It's not over." Seth laughed. "I don't know if you've noticed, but I have a knife against her throat."

Allissa wriggled beneath his grasp. Seth pushed the knife deeper into her skin.

Niki saw the indentation beneath the blade.

"We know who you are, and we know about your great-grandfather."

Seth held Allissa close and dragged her towards the door.

"Just let her go. We can talk about all that later," Niki said.

Allissa tried to speak, but the knife against her throat thwarted any sound.

Seth took another step towards the door. The hem of Allissa's dress dragged through a puddle.

"Let her go."

Another voice echoed from behind Niki. Niki spun around to see Andy hobbling towards them.

"We'll help you," he called out. "We'll make sure you're looked after properly. You'll be able to explain this."

Seth stared at Andy blankly. Then his expression broke into a smile.

"I remember you!" Seth said, laughing as Andy rested on the wall. "You ruined my plans last night. I should do it here and make you watch, just to get my own back."

Niki watched Seth closely. The blade glinted against Allissa's neck.

"I'm sorry I don't have time to chat," Seth said, edging towards the door. "I'm not letting you ruin my fun two nights in a row." Seth was beside the door now. The knife stayed in position as Seth tapped an electronic key on the lock. The lock disengaged.

Andy and Niki watched, waiting for any moment of weakness. The knife was too close to risk it.

Allissa tried to say something. The knife against her throat stymied her words. Seth dragged her backwards again.

"Save your energy." Seth looped his arm around Allissa's neck and pulled her through the door.

"Leo," Allissa muttered.

"He's not here, I'm afraid," Seth said. "It's only me now. We're doing it my way."

The door swung open, and Seth dragged Allissa inside. Niki and Andy stood rooted to the spot. They couldn't move. Seth stepped backwards again. The door swung closed. The lock engaged, trapping Niki and Andy outside.

Seth backed into the foyer. The lights snapped on. The entrance hall was dirty. Three broken bikes languished against one wall. Junk mail skittered across the floor.

Seth moved quickly, dragging Allissa deeper into the building. He reached the back of the foyer, turned left, and disappeared out of Niki's sight.

Niki, dizzy with fear, rushed forwards and tried the door. She pulled it hard. The lock was strong. The door was impenetrable to anyone without a key. She banged on the glass with her fist.

"Someone open this fucking door," she shouted frantically.

87

Leo's heart thumped as he closed the last few hundred yards towards Miller's Court. His legs throbbed. He was wet through from the rain.

He glanced down at the map. Miller's Court was just ahead on the right. The square, grey building cut upwards into the stormy sky.

Leo ran across the road and into the shadowed street. Other than the distant rumble of traffic and the flutter of the pounding rain, everything was quiet. Was he too late? He glanced at the map. He'd run the most direct way. A taxi may have taken a more circuitous route with one-way systems and traffic lights.

Leo staggered into the street. He skirted a pile of rubbish. The outline of the building reared above him. Lights blazed from a few windows. Most were dark. Decrepit letters above the door advertised the building's name — *Miller's Court*.

This was the place.

Leo stepped up to the door and glanced into the gloomy foyer. His breath billowed in great clouds and misted on the frosted glass. A green emergency light washed the place in an eerie glow. It looked like the entrance hall to any other block of flats.

A stream of rain ran inside the collar of Leo's coat. He shuddered.

Leo pulled the door handle. The door didn't move. He swore as he turned to the door entry system's twinkling buttons. Some glowed faintly, and others were dull. The one in the top right corner flickered and then died. Some residents had taped their name beside a button. Flat 13 was blank.

The lights inside the foyer suddenly flickered to life, dazzling him. He squinted through the steamy glass. A grey-haired woman in a long coat shuffled towards the door. A small dog on a lead trotted beside her. She opened the door, muttering to herself, and stepped out into the night.

Leo slid his foot between the door and the frame. The woman walked out without looking back. She disappeared into the gloom, and Leo slipped inside.

The hallway was cold and smelled of damp. Yellowed paper fluttered from a notice board, and a sign on the far wall told Leo to go left for flats 10-15.

Leo turned into the grey-painted corridor. His wet shoes squeaked across the floor.

A bulky radiator clanged. Water dripped from a pipe into a bucket that was almost overflowing.

Leo passed the door for flat 10 on the left and flat 11 on the right.

The building was quiet. A light further down the corridor blinked on and off. On and off.

Leo neared flat 13 and slowed. Every moment he and Allissa had shared led to this. The first time he's seen her in Kathmandu. Their cases in Hong Kong and Berlin. Nights of laughter together on the sagging sofa in their dingy Brighton flat. It all came down to whatever was behind this door.

Leo stopped and studied the door. It was blue like the others with discoloured chrome numbers. The number three's highest screw had failed, causing the number to tilt backwards.

Leo's breathing returned to normal, but his chest ached.

Before meeting Allissa, Leo's anxiety had run riot. He struggled to talk to people on the phone, meet strangers, and sometimes even leave the house. That previous life seemed disconnected from him now, on the trail of a serial killer to save the woman he —

The entrance door slammed behind him, interrupting his thoughts. Leo's head whipped around. The woman with the dog walked back through the foyer and turned the opposite way.

Leo saw Allissa in his mind's eye. Then he saw the killer's blade. He fought for a deep breath. He needed to stay clear-headed and focused now. Everything depended on it. He couldn't let that happen to Allissa.

Leo leant against the door and listened. A slam rang out through the building but flat 13 was silent — as silent as a grave.

The door to the foyer banged open, and footsteps jostled inside. Leo stared towards the noise. Raised voices echoed from the bare walls. Leo recognised Niki's voice.

The door swung closed and Niki's voice sunk. A dull thump reverberated down the hallway as Niki pounded the door.

The footsteps continued towards him. Seth and Allissa were coming his way.

Leo's body tensed and his heart thundered. Seth's footsteps thumped against the floor.

Leo's eyes roamed the corridor for something he could use as a weapon. The corridor was bare. The other flat doors were closed.

Seth's dark silhouette appeared at the end of the corridor. The foyer's strong lights cast a long shadow.

Leo begged himself to act. To move. To fight. Nothing happened. He stood rooted to the spot, watching Seth shuffle closer.

Seth took two steps towards the door. A light snapped on. Leo saw that Seth was facing the other way with his arms wrapped around Allissa. Allissa was struggling but Seth held her tight. He pulled her step by step towards the door. Flat 13 – the scene of his final kill.

Adrenaline whirred through Leo's veins. His focus narrowed on Seth and Allissa. He stepped away from them silently on the balls of his feet. He wanted to let Seth and Allissa get into the flat. Seth would be trapped in there. Leo also assumed Seth would release Allissa for a moment to lock the door. That would be his time to attack.

A recessed doorway at the end of the corridor led into a fire escape. Leo pushed his back flat against the door and peered out. Seth and Allissa reached the door of flat 13.

Seth twisted Allissa around as though she were already lifeless. Leo watched silently from fifteen feet away. The blade of Seth's knife flashed in the light. Seth pressed the knife into Allissa's neck. Her face was a mask of fear. Her eyes were wide, and her mouth was set in a thin grimace.

Leo watched. His pulse galloped. His stomach was a fist of iron.

Seth drew a key from his pocket, and then slid it into the

lock. The knife remained at Allissa's throat throughout. He turned the key and pushed the door open.

Seth glanced around the corridor. His face contorted into an animalistic grin.

Leo, barely concealed in the recessed fire escape, pushed his back into the door to remain out of sight. The door clunked and swung open. A draft of cold air swept into the corridor. Leo grabbed the frame to prevent himself from falling backwards. His eyes sprang wide open and his breath caught in his throat.

Seth's eyes homed in on the noise. He tilted his head to the side and examined the empty corridor. He held Allissa still. For long seconds he didn't even blink.

Leo held his breath and cowered out of sight. The door behind Leo swung and thumped closed again.

Seth looked from the empty corridor to the open door of flat 13. He grinned, removed the knife from Allissa's neck and shoved her inside. Then he stepped inside too and slammed the door.

88

Allissa stumbled forwards into the darkened room. Her feet slipped across the floor. She reached out and steadied herself on the wall.

She drew a deep breath and tried to calm herself. Getting into a state of panic wouldn't help at all. She ran a finger across her neck. She could still feel the blade of Seth's knife against her skin.

She cursed herself for not seeing this coming. *How could I have been so stupid?*

Allissa stood up straight and exhaled. Her heart thundered relentlessly. She needed to think clearly. She was not a lamb to the slaughter. She was not giving up. She planted her feet firmly on the floor, tried to forget the sensation of the blade against her skin, and turned around.

Seth turned the key in the lock. The knife remained in his right hand. With the precise movements of a maniac, he removed the key and tucked it back inside his pocket. He switched on the light and looked at Allissa. His eyes were dark, unblinking and malevolent.

Allissa returned his stare. Her muscles tensed and a thin

film of sweat mottled her brow. It was oppressively warm in the small room.

Seth raised the knife and pointed it towards Allissa.

"I'm so pleased you've decided to join me," he said, standing with his back to the door. "I've been keeping this place a secret for so long. It's wonderful to be able to share it with someone as extraordinary as you." Seth's eyes scanned Allissa's body.

Allissa ignored the wave of repulsion which roared through her. She used Seth's momentary distraction to glance around the room. The more she knew about the place, the better chance she stood. It was a simple one-room flat. A bed with a bare, stained mattress sat against one wall. The surge of disgust returned as Allissa considered what Seth planned on using that for. Allissa forced herself to focus. Focus could be the difference between life and death. A kitchenette occupied the other end of the room and a door led through to what Allissa assumed was the bathroom.

"Well," Seth continued, "you'll be extraordinary once I've finished with you. We're going down in history together."

Allissa noticed a framed picture on the wall behind Seth. It was a large sepia-toned photograph of an eccentric looking man with a huge moustache.

"That's my great-grandfather," Seth said. His voice was little more than a whisper now. He extended the knife towards Allissa. "I think you'll be familiar with his work."

Allissa glanced from the photograph to Seth and back again.

"I've never seen him before," she replied defiantly.

Seth swept his hair back out of his face with his free hand. The knife stayed directed at Allissa.

"Mary Ann Nichols, Annie Chapman, Elizabeth Stride, Catherine Eddowes —"

"And Mary Jane Kelly," Allissa interrupted. "Jack the Ripper."

"Clever girl."

"You think you can do better, is that what this is?" The murders lined up with awful finality in Allissa's mind.

"Not do better," Seth said. "Rather, pay homage."

Seth was interrupted by an ear-splitting crash. The door splintered and sprung open.

89

"We've got to get inside," Niki shouted, pulling desperately on the door.

Andy limped across to the door entrance system and started thumbing the buttons. There were about sixty flats in the building. One of the residents had to be in.

"Come on." Niki yanked the door again. She didn't dare think about what might be going on inside. "Where the fuck is Leo?"

Andy pressed the first twenty doorbells, one after another. He paused and peered into the foyer. There was no answer. He started again.

Niki stepped out into the pounding rain and glanced up at the flats. Most of the windows were dark.

"Come on, come on," she whispered, looking back at the door. An emergency exit light washed the foyer in an eerie glow. Niki bit her lip, her brow furrowed. Her hands clenched into fists. The growl of the city had now sunk beneath the pattering rain. A siren moaned from somewhere far away. Niki had the awful feeling they weren't coming this way.

A distant crash echoed through the building. Niki charged back towards the glass and peered in. Her eyes swept the foyer frantically.

This was more than business now. This was life and death.

"What you want?" came a disembodied voice, straining from the speaker beside the door.

The voice caught Niki by surprise. Andy turned to face her. Niki's mouth stumbled over unsaid words.

"Hello?" came the voice again. "What you want?"

Niki jumped towards the speaker. She thought about all the things she could say to get access to the building. Over her years in detection she'd tried many. One always worked the best.

"Pizza," she mumbled in a deep voice.

There was silence on the line.

"I didn't order pizza," the voice replied.

"Someone has. Want it or not?"

The door buzzed open.

90

Leo stalked down the corridor towards flat 13. His eyes narrowed on the discoloured door. His muscles rippled with tension. Allissa was inside that room with a man who'd killed multiple times. A man with a taste for blood.

Leo took the final few steps on the balls of his feet. He held his breath, afraid that any sound would give his position away.

The corridor was silent. Rain rattled against the glass doors of the foyer. Leo considered going to let Niki and Andy in. Surging adrenaline reminded him that time was too short.

He leant close to the door and listened. Seth's muffled voice strained from inside. Leo heard Allissa reply and relief swelled through his body. It gave him a physical boost of power. He wasn't too late.

Leo examined the door. Although he'd heard Seth's key grate in the lock, the door was flimsy. The mechanism looked rickety and weak. A firm shoulder would get that open in moments. Leo glanced up and down the corridor.

He tried to swallow but couldn't. His mouth tasted dry and metallic.

An image of Allissa flashed into Leo's mind.

Leo took a step back and rubbed his hands together. They were sweaty despite the cold. Leo practised the twisting motion he would need to barge the door with his shoulder. He dropped into a crouch.

His pulse hurtled on. He pulled a deep breath. Then, he charged for the door.

Pain shot through Leo's body as the door clattered open. A shout echoed through the room.

The door smashed into Seth and knocked him off balance. He stumbled towards the bed.

Leo grabbed hold of the doorframe to stop himself falling. He steadied himself quickly and glanced around.

Seth caught his footing and spun to face Leo. He raised the knife and snarled.

Allissa looked from Seth to Leo. Her eyes were wide with fear. She took a small step away from Seth.

Leo took in the room. The bed, the kitchenette, the photograph hanging on the wall.

"This isn't the way it's supposed to go." Seth's eyes roamed from Leo to Allissa. "It doesn't matter. I'll make do."

Leo's hands squeezed into fists. He was ready for Seth's attack.

It took Leo less than a heartbeat to make a decision. Allissa was going to walk away from that room, even if he had to go down with the maniac. Leo would stop this killer, even if it cost him everything. He sunk into a crouch and gazed intently into Seth's wild eyes.

Seth looked back at Leo. He swung the knife through the air and breathed deeply. His lips parted into a grimace.

Then he turned and charged for Allissa. The knife swished from left to right, its deadly blade singing through the air.

Leo turned and grabbed the framed photograph from the wall. He tore it from its fixing. The wooden frame was heavy.

Allissa backed away, avoiding Seth's blade by inches.

Seth moved forward again. His eyes shone in manic determination. He lunged forward and grabbed a fist full of Allissa's hair. Seth held the knife high. His muscles tensed for the downward stroke.

Allissa screamed and lashed out. She was a writhing ball of energy.

Seth pulled Allissa's hair harder. Allissa kicked him. The pain meant nothing. Seth was wholly focused on finishing the job. Seth pulled Allissa's head backwards, exposing her throat.

Allissa delivered two punches to Seth's midriff. No reaction.

Seth's jaw clenched. His muscles tightened. The knife swung through the air, approaching Allissa's neck.

Leo's heart roared. His lungs stung. His muscles tingled with expectation. His brain thronged under adrenaline's spell.

Leo wrapped his hands around the edge of the frame and raised it over his left shoulder. He charged forwards and swung the picture at Seth's outstretched arm. Time moved slowly. Each heartbeat a victory. Each movement a marathon.

Seth's knife moved down. It was just inches from Allissa's exposed throat now.

Allissa cried out and tried to move.

Seth pulled her hair even harder.

Allissa struck him in the chin and again in the stomach. He didn't even blink.

Leo threw his weight behind the photograph's solid wooden frame.

Seth was so focused on Allissa and the knife that he didn't see it coming.

The frame smashed into Seth's forearm with an ear-splitting crack.

Seth's eyes widened in surprise and then clamped shut in pain. His forearm bent at an unnatural angle. The knife spun from his hand. He screamed. Seth opened his eyes and examined his forearm. He let go of Allissa's hair and wrapped his left hand around his damaged arm.

The knife clanged away across the floor.

Leo charged on and smashed the frame into Seth again. It thumped into the back of Seth's skull. Glass shattered. Seth howled and dropped to the floor.

Leo lifted the frame to attack again. He wouldn't stop until this man was —

"No, no, stop," Allissa said, grabbing Leo's arm. "The police will be here soon."

Leo dropped the frame, crouched over Seth and pinned him to the floor. Seth flailed about, trying to shake Leo off. Leo grabbed Seth's uninjured arm and pushed it up behind his back.

Allissa kicked the knife away.

"My arm, my fucking arm!"

"I'll break the other one too," Leo snarled. Anger boiled through his veins.

Allissa glanced at Leo. A strange feeling welled through her. It was something like intense gratitude, but more. She suppressed it and looked around the room.

"Hey, look at that," Allissa said, and pointed the wall where the picture had been.

There was a hollow in the wall and some items were stashed inside.

"Touch that and I'll fucking kill you," Seth said, writhing again.

Leo pushed Seth's arm higher behind his back. Leo's boiling rage was subsiding now.

Allissa pulled the items from the hollow and dropped them to the bed. There was a thick roll of banknotes and a passport.

"You going somewhere?" Allissa said, looking at Seth. She looked at Leo and her expression melted into a smile.

"What's happening?" came a voice from the door. Niki charged into the room followed by Andy.

Seth lashed out and tried to stand. Leo pushed Seth's head against the cracked concrete floor.

The red and white lights of a police car strobed through the thin curtains. The noise of sirens cut through the rain.

"Oh shit. You've got him!" Niki said.

"Yeah," Allissa replied, sliding the roll of banknotes into her pocket. "Well, Leo did."

EPILOGUE

"Where were you when this happened?" Allissa asked. "Do you remember?"

"Yes, I do," Leo said. "I was on the bus on the way back from school. The radio was on, and it was all over the news. I didn't really understand what was happening until I got home and saw it on the telly."

They were standing at the railing of the 9/11 Memorial in Lower Manhattan. Two pools sunk deep into the ground marked the location where the towers once stood. Water trickled down the sides, giving the pools an impression of infinity. The walls surrounding the pools displayed the names of the dead.

People moved around slowly, each wrapped in thick coats and scarves against the winter chill. Some read the names, and others gazed at the sky. A group of school children in matching red hats followed their teacher towards the South Tower.

"How do you feel about going home?" Leo asked. They'd booked their flights for the following day.

New York

Two days had passed since Seth's arrest. After the police had arrived and Andy was taken back to the hospital, Leo and Allissa returned to their hotel room where they'd slept for nearly eighteen hours. After the day's harrowing events, Allissa had doubted she'd be able to sleep. But, in the comfort of her bed in their Chinatown hotel room, she sunk quickly into luscious dreamlessness. She knew the memory would live on — the cold steel against her throat. She also knew that without what she, Leo, Niki and Andy had done, a killer would have remained at large.

"Yeah, I'm excited about it," Allissa said, gazing across the pool. "We're definitely having some time off now. I don't care what comes up." She ran a gloved hand across her throat.

"For sure," Leo said. "With that money we can have at least a couple of weeks off."

Andy, Leo and Allissa had split the money they'd found behind the picture in apartment 13. They all agreed there was no point giving it to the police.

"It's a good opportunity for him to look after Emma and Frankie," Leo said, thinking out loud. "If he uses it to fill himself with booze, though, there'll be trouble."

"He said he wouldn't drink again."

"Yes, he did," Leo agreed, "and that's a great start. I just hope he can actually do it."

Allissa nodded. "Maybe we should stay in England for a couple of months just to keep an eye on them."

"I'd like that, actually."

Leo and Allissa took a step back to let an older couple pass. They read each of the names and then paused for a moment before moving on to the next.

"Hey, look who it is." Allissa pointed across the pool.

Leo followed Allissa's gaze and saw Niki Zadid standing at the railing. Her hands rested on one of the inscribed names. Her blue headscarf trembled in the breeze. Her lips moved as she whispered something. Then, as quickly as she appeared, she turned and walked away.

"Come on," Allissa said, "let's go and see —"

Leo was about to argue, but Allissa had already stepped away.

Allissa reached the point where Niki had been standing and scanned the names.

"Look," Allissa said as Leo caught up, "right there."

"Hassan Zadid," Leo read.

"We'd only been married six months," came a voice from behind them. Leo and Allissa spun to see Niki behind them.

"I was nineteen and he was twenty-one when we married. Then this happened." Niki stepped between Leo and Allissa and touched the inscribed name.

"I'm sorry, I had no idea," Allissa said.

"Why would you?" Niki's hazelnut eyes considered her. "He'd only been working here a few months." Niki dabbed at her eyes, then disguised it by straightening her headscarf. "It's just one of those things. I was studying law at the time, but soon after qualifying I realised my heart just wasn't in it. I needed to do something different, something for me."

Niki led them away from the memorial. She stopped and glanced from Allissa to Leo and back again. "Just make sure you're not wasting time. If there's something you gotta do, then you gotta do it."

Leo gazed into Niki's eyes. Allissa nodded.

"When are you guys off?" Niki asked, her voice lightening as her lopsided smile returned.

"Tomorrow," Allissa said.

Leo stood in silence. Niki's words tumbled through his mind.

"Oh gosh, tomorrow?" Niki said, dissolving back into her larger-than-life persona. "Well, you've got loads to see and you don't wanna waste your time chatting here. Where you heading?"

"Not sure," Leo said, "we've heard the High Line's worth a visit."

"Sure is," Niki said. "It's a bit of a walk, but for you young things that'll be fine. Head that way and just keep going."

"Thanks," Leo said. "And thanks, you know, for your help with finding Andy."

"Anytime," Niki said, "and if you're ever back over here, look me up for sure."

"We will."

Niki and Allissa hugged. Allissa then turned and walked in the direction Niki had indicated.

Leo and Niki stared at each other.

"Do it," Niki whispered, an additional glimmer in her eyes.

Leo forced a nervous smile and hurried after Allissa.

The afternoon was getting colder now. People rushed with their collars turned up against the chill. Leo and Allissa walked in silence for a few minutes.

"This place reminds me of what you said that night in St Lucia," Allissa said, looking at Leo beside her.

"What's that?"

"You said that our lives were like a film. It really feels like it walking around here, don't you think?"

"I suppose," Leo agreed.

"You never answered my question that night, either."

Leo couldn't remember the question.

"Who do you think would play you if our lives were a film?" She tapped Leo on the arm.

Leo inhaled a chest full of the cool winter air.

Do it.

He let the air fill his lungs, feed his courage, then let it go slowly. He gazed at the surrounding buildings, then turned to Allissa.

Their hands fell together like the last leaves of autumn.

"Who would play me?" Leo looked down at the woman he'd literally followed to the ends of the earth. He paused as he remembered how afraid he'd been to lose her. Now he couldn't even imagine their lives apart.

In his mind's eye, the final scene of a movie played out. Strings rose to their climax, the camera zoomed out, and dust danced in the projector's beam.

"I'd play me," Leo said, moving his hand to Allissa's waist. "If you promised to play you."

As Leo leant forwards, three things happened at once.

First, one of those moments occurred where the present leaves the past behind. Things divide neatly. They reinvent themselves in a wave of paradigm-shifting realisations.

Second, the first flakes of the coming winter snow scattered amongst the towers.

And third, a figure peered out from behind a building and watched them.

Niki saw them, smiled her lopsided smile, straightened her headscarf and walked toward Greenwich Village.

Leo and Allissa's next case will take them to Riga

I'm in the process of writing Leo & Allissa's next case, in which they'll go to the Latvian capital, Riga.

New York

I visited Riga in the autumn of 2020, and have wanted to write about it ever since.

Pre-order today to make sure you get your copy as soon as it's released.

www.lukerichardsonauthor.com/riga

WHAT HAPPENED IN KOH TAO?

Read the series prequel novella for free now:
www.lukerichardsonauthor.com/kohtao

"Intense, thrilling, mysterious and captivating."

"The story grabs you, you're on the boat with your stomach pitching. As the story gathers pace the tension is palpable. It's a page turner which keeps you hooked until the final word."

"The evocative writing takes you to a place of white sand, the turquoise sea and tranquilly. But on an island of injustice and exploitation, tranquillity is the last thing Leo finds."

"Love and adventure collide in Thailand, love it!"

KOH TAO

Leo's looking for the perfect place to propose to the love of his life. When they arrive in the Thai tropical paradise of Koh Tao, he thinks he's found it.

But before he gets an answer, she's nowhere to be seen.

On searching the resort, his tranquillity turns to turmoil. Is it a practical joke? Has she run away? Or is it something much more sinister?

Set two years before Luke Richardson's international thriller series, this compulsive novella turns back the clock on an anxiety ridden man battling powerful forces in a foreign land.

KOH TAO is the prequel novella to Luke Richardson's international thriller series. Grab your copy for free and find out where it all began!

www.lukerichardsonauthor.com/kohtao

*As always, this book is dedicated to those I travel beside.
Especially Martha, Alicia and George. My favourite journey is
coming home to you.*

JOIN MY MAILING LIST

During the years it took me to write plan and this book, I always looked to its publication as being the end of the process. The book would be out, and the story would be finished.

Since releasing it in May 2019, I realised that putting the book into the world was actually just the start. Now I go on the adventure with every conversation I have about it. It's so good to hear people's frustrations with Leo's reserve, their shock at the truth about the grizzly backstreet restaurant, and their questions about what's going to happen next.

Most of these conversations happen with people on my mailing list, and I'd love you to join too.

I send an email a couple of times a month in which I talk about my new releases, my inspirations and my travels.

Sign up now:

www.lukerichardsonauthor.com/mailinglist

OTHER BOOKS BY LUKE RICHARDSON

Leo & Allissa International Thrillers

Koh Tao
www.lukerichardsonauthor.com/kohtao

Kathmandu
www.lukerichardsonauthor.com/kathmandu

Hong Kong
www.lukerichardsonauthor.com/hongkong

Berlin
www.lukerichardsonauthor.com/berlin

New York
www.lukerichardsonauthor.com/newyork

Riga
www.lukerichardsonauthor.com/riga

The Liberator: Kayla Stone Vigilante Thrillers

Justice is her beat

Her name is Kayla Stone

She is 'The Liberator'

The Liberator Series is a ferocious new collaboration between Luke Richardson and Amazon Bestseller, Steven Moore.

If you like Clive Cussler, Nick Thacker, Ernest Dempsey and Rusesel Blake, then you'll love this explosive new series!

www.lukerichardsonauthor.com/theliberator

THANK YOU

Thank you for reading *New York*. Sharing my writing with you has been a dream of many years. Thank you for making it a reality.

As may come across in my writing, travelling, exploring and seeing the world is so important to me, as is coming home to my family and friends.

Although the words here are my own, the characters, experiences and some of the events described are wholly inspired by the people I've travelled beside. If we shared noodles from a street-food vendor, visited a temple together, played cards on a creaking overnight train, or had a beer in a back-street restaurant, you are forever in this book.

It is the intention of my writing to show that although the world is big and the unknown can be unsettling, there is so much good in it. Although some of the people in my stories are bad and evil — the story wouldn't be very interesting if they weren't — they're vastly outnumbered by the honesty, purity and kindness of the other characters. You don't have to look far to see this in the real world. I know that whenever I travel, it's the kindness of the people that I

Thank you

remember almost more than the place itself. Whether you're an experienced traveller, or you prefer your home turf, it's my hope that this story has taken you somewhere new and exciting.

Again, thank you for coming on the adventure with me. I hope to see you again soon.

Luke

PS. A little warning, next time someone talks to you in the airport, be careful what you say, as you may end up in their book.

BOOK REVIEWS

If you've enjoyed this book I would appreciate a review.

Reviews are essential for three reasons. Firstly, they encourage people to take a chance on an author they've never heard of. Secondly, bookselling websites use them to decide what books to recommend through their search engine. And third, I love to hear what you think!

Having good reviews really can make a massive difference to new authors like me.

It'll take you no longer than two minutes, and will mean the world to me.

www.lukerichardsonauthor.com/reviews

Thank you.

Printed in Great Britain
by Amazon